D1259231

THE FAMILY MAN

THE
FAMILY MAN

JOSEPH MONNINGER

NEW YORK
ATHENEUM
1982

ASBURY PARK PUBLIC LIBRARY
ASBURY PARK, NEW JERSEY

Library of Congress Cataloging in Publication Data

Monninger, Joseph.
The family man.

I. Title.
PS3563.0526F3   813'.54   81–12870
ISBN 0–689–11235–1   AACR2

Copyright © 1982 by Joseph Monninger
All rights reserved
Published simultaneously in Canada by
McClelland and Stewart Ltd.
Composition by American–Stratford Graphic Services, Inc.,
Brattleboro, Vermont
Manufactured by Fairfield Graphics, Fairfield, Pennsylvania
Designed by Mary Cregan
First Edition

to my father,
CHARLES F. MONNINGER

———

For when it is quite, quite nothing, then it is everything.

D. H. LAWRENCE
New Heaven and Earth

THE FAMILY MAN

1

I look out at the yard and I am smitten by the sight of a lurking, charcoal-soiled, freewheeling, easy-cook, superchef barbecue grill. It is not a pleasant sight. I can hear the sound of my wife cooking in the kitchen. Here in our living room rest three five-hundred-dollar chairs that are too expensive to sit in. They are left alone in a silent tribute to money and to the effect it can have on friends. In the rec room my two children are watching television.

"Peter, would you like carrots or potatoes with the steak?" Jill asks.

I have no answer. I think either would be fine. Perhaps the two would be nice together. You could grind the carrots into the potatoes and make a sort of vegetable mash out of them.

"Carrots, dear."

"Oh, Peter, you know the kids hate carrots."

"Then let's have potatoes."

"All right, are you sure?"

"Yes."

More clanking in the kitchen. It takes so little to make

those you love happy. My children will be happy tonight at dinner. They will know that the potatoes are for them. They will know that they are only a few brief minutes away from another hour in front of the TV set. I get up and go into the kitchen. There is rain in the air and I need coffee to warm me. I would like to smell it more than drink it. I try to fix it myself, but my wife insists. She looks quickly in the direction of the rec room and then leans over and pecks me on the lips. We are apparently living in sin. I shouldn't like my children to know my wife and I kiss occasionally. It would be too un-Catholic, which we are, and too trumped up, which it is.

I don't love my wife anymore. I feel the same affection for her as I did for my childhood dog, which I named Peter, after myself. He looked fine when he came in from the rain with his hair matted to his sides and the odor of bone on his breath. We'd lie on the kitchen floor and watch my mother cook. She was a poor woman who met trains for a living. My father was a commuter on the New Jersey Central. Every day my mother took him to and from the station. Sometimes she would wait for hours, until it became obvious that either the train was absurdly late or it had crashed and my father was dead. Then she would rush home and call up the train line. They would feed her the news and she would hang up the phone, repeating thank-yous like Hail Marys on a rosary.

"You'd better get the fire started," my wife says to me.

I take the coffee out into the evening air. Clouds hang on the shoulders of neighboring houses. The charcoal is hard to light. I splash some lighter fluid on it and watch a match explode. My cigarette blends into the taste of the coffee.

4

The lawn is soft and shaggy. A soft wind kicks up and carries the smell of the barbecue to the farthest end of the neighborhood. The people next door are block parents. If my children, anyone's children, are lost or being raped, they can go to the block parents' house. Children have nothing to be afraid of there. For providing this service, the people get to hang a shield in their window.

"Is it going to rain?" my wife calls out.

"It might."

"Can you take the grill into the garage?"

"If it rains."

"Okay, dear."

Everything is okay. Everything. The steak will be cooked to a turn. A shot of whiskey would have gone well in this coffee. We have strayed away from cocktail drinking. Habit-forming, time-consuming, and nonproductive. An ounce of alcohol kills a zillion brain cells. Always the same message: We are eating and smoking ourselves to death. A few rain-drops splatter. The fire crackles, ready to do battle.

"You'd better get the grill inside," she warns through the kitchen window.

"I will."

I wheel the grill into the garage. The door is open and the smoke moves quietly out. The rain closes me off like a a curtain. The asphalt of the driveway is wet and sparkling. A breeze comes up and I move the grill a bit farther inside. There is nothing now to prevent a happy outcome. The steaks will be done, and the potatoes ready. The four of us will sit down and replenish our bodies. A small figure hurries out the back door. It is covered by my raincoat and there is something in its hand.

5

"Here's the steak, Dad."

My son and I are alone out here. The house is something far away. I look at my boy and wonder what he'll be. I want him to be something I don't yet understand. But there is no telling; there is no saying.

"You hungry, Ron?" I ask.

"A little."

"Well, wait till you smell this on the fire."

The steak sizzles and bites as I place it on the grill.

"Did you get those summer reading books read yet?"

"No."

"School's only a couple of weeks off."

"I know, Dad."

There must be more to say. I sip my coffee and look out at the driveway. Little currents of water are skidding along nicely. My son is uneasy and anxious. I can tell he would rather be inside.

"Where's your sister?"

"In helping Mom."

"Kind of nice, just us two being out here, huh?"

"Yeah, Dad."

The night seems to be shouting at us. The steak drips grease on the fire. A flame shoots up and I temper it by sprinkling fingertips of coffee.

"Your birthday's coming up, isn't it?"

"Yeah."

A short glimmer. A type of classical conditioning that I play on. His eyes are brown, like mine. His hair is soft and light; the wind throws it back and forth. This should be a fuller moment between us. There is the rain and the wind.

"Well, what would you like?" I ask.

6

"I don't know yet."

"Last year wasn't it a hockey stick?"

"Yep."

"We'll have to go into the city for a Rangers game one of these days, huh?"

"Sure, Dad."

"We didn't play hockey when I was a kid."

"What did you play?"

"Mostly stickball. Sometimes when we got enough guys together, we'd play hardball. I remember one time . . ."

"Ronald, come in here for a minute please," his mother calls from the kitchen.

A rushing off and the boy is gone. Eleven years old and his leaving makes me empty. I think of my father and wonder how the dirt lies on his eyes. I am sure the casket gave way long ago. His gray mustache must be probing his upper gums by now. There is no lightning tonight. Only the soft sweep of rain on a summer evening.

"Mom says to tell you the potatoes are done." He is back.

"All right. Tell her I'm taking up the steak."

Ron running off again. He hunches over and hides from the rain. I would like to be inside his sneakers, to feel the soft squish of water in his socks. I lift the steak a final time and watch the flames reach up to reclaim it. I stick it on a metal plate and see the blood run into the little grooves put there to collect it. My daughter likes the blood on her bread. She sprinkles garlic salt on it and eats it with her fingers. I carry the steak into the house. The family gathers around to sniff.

"Don't you think it should stay on a shade longer?" my wife asks.

"Do you?"

"Yes."

"Then why did you ask?"

"I was only trying—"

I cut out before the sentence is completed. Throw the steak back on the fire. I see the delightful red being consumed by heat. We will have well-done steak. We will have moccasin brown steak. I no longer aim toward perfection; I let things go as they must. When the steak has to be done, I lift it and put it back on the plate. Inside, I set the platter down and see that my wife is ready to accept it this time no matter what. Because really, the potatoes are done.

"Good. Children, dinner's ready," she calls.

Feet hustling to the table. My wife takes orders for drinks. I ask for milk but am told it is for breakfast. I settle for Kool-Aid and the kids follow suit. My wife and I once drank wine at meals, but it proved too expensive. I would end up slightly drunk and my wife would end up slightly angry. Such are the little crimes of marriage.

"Won't you carve, darling?" she asks.

God, that I were a darling, a cherub. It is a mockery and the kids know it. Ron sits to my right and Lori to my left. I chop up the meat and we join hands. Religion is my wife's responsibility. She thinks children need religion the way they need clean socks.

"God is good, God is great, let us thank Him for our food. Amen."

Clatter of knives and forks. The children look at each other's slices, trying to determine who's more in my favor these days.

"Knock-knock," Ron says.

"Who's there?" Lori falls for it.

"John."

"John who?"

"John the Baptist."

Ron flicks water at Lori. I think it a little funny. Table manners are to be remembered, however. I try to stretch my mind to fit into place. I was a literature major in college. My wife quit a career in nursing to launch me in an uncle's accounting firm. We were a model couple. We agreed early in our marriage that we needed only to be replaced on this earth. "Two is all," she said firmly. "But"—and I always like to ask her this—"what if one dies?"

"Children, sit up straight."

They manage to sit like poles. Their backs are liquid granite. There is no latitude at this meal. Ron drops a fork on the floor and bends under the table to get it. Lori looks under, too, and they both come up laughing.

"Pass the potatoes, please," Lori says.

Hands carry the bowl forward. Lori daintily pokes one onto her plate. There is enough blood gathered in the grooves of the steak platter for her bread and garlic salt now. I dunk a piece and hand it to her with my pinkie extended.

"Peter, we have silverware."

We do, but we use the utensils we got at the supermarket with our boxes of laundry soap. The silverware is for company.

"We have ice cream and chocolate cake for dessert," she announces when we have finished.

A favorite combination. The dry warmth of the cake sends feelers into the ice cream. My wife and Lori bring out

9

small plates. The girls hand us dainty forks. We are eating at a doll's table.

"A big slice, Peter?"

"Not too big."

"Big enough?"

She moves the knife along the rim of the cake in an attempt to show me just how much she is willing to give me. I want to tell her it is not enough—nothing she could give me would be enough. She passes me the slice and watches me chew it down. There is pride in her eyes. I like the cake. It is even better than the steak.

"Can I have another piece, Mom?" Ron asks.

Her eyes glow. This is a mother's moment. She gives Ron a dab more.

"What are you going to do about the grill?" she asks me.

I don't know. It can't stay in the garage next to the car. It would be too dangerous. I will have to wheel it out to the back garden and pour the powdery flame on the rose bed. I think of the night lingering outside and it seems dark and distant.

"You kids get your pajamas on."

The kids scurry off and we are alone.

"The kids are getting older, aren't they?" she remarks.

We seldom get younger, but these children's growing up means something. It carries weight for both of us. We find beauty in their aging and death in ours.

"I wish you'd get to the shutters soon. They're becoming a sight."

Gray shutters chipped away to cinders. They look shoddy against the white backdrop of the recently painted house. It hurts the neighborhood's appearance. I lick the plate and come away with a glob of icing. It floats to the top of my mouth and sticks there. I let it dissolve in a slow, sensual movement. My wife watches with delight. She sees something sexy there. I scoop up a little more icing and rub it on my teeth. I smile at her and she groans at the chocolaty darkness.

"Can we watch TV?" The children reappear.

"Are your rooms clean?" Jill asks.

"Yes."

"All right."

The little bobbins hop off. They look downy in their pj's. We have been at the table too long. My wife seems restless and bored. I attempt small talk, but it is too small. What we need is a good drop of gossip stirred in. Other people's lives are more important to us than our own. In the next room I can hear the TV. It sounds warm and homey. I can picture the kids' faces as they bask in the rays. Their eyes flicker and blink.

"I'll put away the grill."

I walk out to the night. A breeze passes, the hint of autumn riding on its back. I suck in deep gulps of air and light a cigarette. The smoke is riddled with holes by the plunging rain.

> O Western wind, when wilt thou blow,
> That the small rain down can rain?
> Christ, if my love were in my arms
> And I in my bed again!

A remembered stanza among the many forgotten. One sweep of feeling as deep and still as the night. We came from nowhere to go nowhere. I am alone. I lead the grill out into the rain and watch as the coals turn black. The grill will rust from the rain, but for the moment it doesn't matter. I want more of this night. I walk slowly back among the birch trees. A wind sends drops showering down on me. Trees bend to one another, whispering. They know I am an intruder. They know I am lost.

"Peter, where are you?"

My wife is searching for me. I hide behind one of the trees. She is looking into the gloom of the night.

"Peter?"

"Boo!" I jump out and canter up to her. She is appalled but charmed by my boyishness. There is little I can do to please her. We are unequals in an unequal world.

"You scared me to death."

"I'm sorry."

"You were taking so long."

"Come on, let's take a walk."

"The children?"

"Let them watch TV."

"Oh, Peter."

A sigh and a whiff of clean hair. I stroke it and hold it close. Her head fits the mold of my shoulder. I have learned to tuck my chin over the crown of her head. The rain picks up. I realize somewhere deep inside that the storm is in its death throes. It rattles on the silence in each of us. There is an unsureness about our own durability. I have spent fourteen years of my life with this one person.

"I'm going inside. Coming?" she asks.

Inside, we go into the rec room. The children are scattered on the floor. There is something essential in their reclining when they watch TV. I would like to sweep them all up in a Monopoly game, but it is almost bedtime.

"Look," Lori says.

A baby lion nuzzles against his mother's stomach. At a glance I can tell he is hungry. His mother ignores him and continues looking at the camera. Another lion cub comes into the picture and begins to wrestle with the first. In the background we get sun-faded pictures of the African savanna. The bent and twisted trees shimmer in the dry heat. There is an old man's voice telling us what we are seeing is nature at its best. The children are engrossed. Lori says the lion looks like a kitty. It is a con job, but we all ooh and ahh at her innocence anyway. She is too sweet for words. I pick up a magazine that is near my chair. It is a family journal that depicts typical family scenes. There is no photograph of a TV set. I turn to look at the clock and see that it is exactly bedtime. We will put the rascals to bed. My wife and I will be alone. She will turn to me and I will light a cigarette.

"Good night, Daddy."

My sweet little girl. She is all goodness and grace. I kiss her on the cheek and hug to me. She is woman-warm. The boy follows and says good night in a stand-offish way. I want to kneel down in front of him, beg him to come closer. Our eyes meet and I release him. He is gone in a flash. Up the stairs the feet thud on. I used to attend last-minute prayer sayings. Now I leave it to my wife and the God that exists or doesn't. There is no room for a middleman in prayers. I hear my wife whispering good nights. She walks down the hall and pauses at the steps.

"Mom, leave the hall light on." Lori calls.

The girl is afraid of the night. The boy is too, but he

wouldn't admit it. The rain is dying on the roof. I hear the slow drip of the gutter outside. My wife is now at the foot of the steps. I hear her glide into the rec room and turn off the TV. The new-won silence is overwhelming. I open the kitchen door and gaze out into the night. Bugs cluster on the screen only to shoot off again at the light.

"Let's have a drink, Peter."

This is unusual. I go to the coat closet and bring down a bottle of scotch. It is dusty but not old. We sit at the kitchen table and stare at each other. There is a world of things to say. I pour two drinks and fetch a bottle of soda from beneath the sink. My wife looks tired. Her hair is frazzled and her clothes seem to stick to her body.

"Peter, what is it?"

"What's what?"

"What is it? You seem so restless."

"I am."

"Don't you want to talk about it?"

"Sure."

"Well?"

"It's nothing."

"But it is. I could feel it all evening."

"Probably the weather."

"It is not and you know it. Tell me."

"I'm just worn-out."

"From work?"

"From everything."

"You seem angry with me. I think the children sense it."

"I can't help their sensing things. It's good training for life."

"Stop it, Peter."

14

"But it is."

"Stop it!"

I stop everything. I hold my breath and let my eyes bug out. She watches without laughing. This should have brought humor to us. There is something upset in her.

"Let's go to bed, Peter. I'm tired."

We walk up the stairs together. The glasses of scotch wait in the kitchen. It will be eight hours before we come back to them. At the top of the stairs I reach to turn off the light and then I remember the kids. We stop at the bedroom door and look down the long, dim hallway. The light is only enough to show us the children's doors. I strain to hear sounds of their breathing. The house groans softly.

"They're asleep," Jill says.

We walk into the bedroom. A practiced hand flicks on the switch. The bed seems to occupy too much space. I step into the bathroom to be away from it. The sink and shower stall are a tired purple. A throw rug stretches lazily on the floor. I splash water on my face. I can taste the tobacco on my lips. From the cup holder I extract my toothbrush and use it. I make sure I am loud enough so my wife will hear. As soon as I am done, I want another cigarette. There is no predicting these things. I walk into the bedroom and see my wife wearing the dark blue robe. Her hair is undone and it falls smoothly over her shoulders. I feel a moment of sexual desire, but it fades faster than it came. I lie down on the bed and light a cigarette. This is a movie moment.

"Shall I put in the diaphragm?" she asks.

"It's really up to you."

"It's up to both of us," she replies. "I can put it in, but let's not feel as if we have to."

15

I nod. She moves to her dresser and takes a blue case out of her top drawer. It fits secretively in her palm. She walks to the bathroom and closes the door. I try to imagine her inserting it. She is alone in there while I wait out here. The rubber circle keeps us farther apart. The door swings open again and she is there.

She takes off her robe and drapes it over the back of a chair. With swift, sure movements she makes her way to the bed. I turn off the lamp and she climbs in beside me.

"We need to just hold each other," she says to me.

"I know."

Her warm body presses to me. I feel hot with her so close. I get up and open the two windows. A cool cross breeze filters through the room. I look out the window and think how free the night is. Behind me the bed is waiting. I climb back in and place my arm around her neck. She lifts her head and rests it on my chest. We blend quietly, but there is no progress. We both could fall asleep without regret. I move a hand to the side of her breast. She responds, but it is all within reason. We are more and more reasonable each night. We are infinitely polite. We are correct in every move and gesture. It is a tenderness we've bought from the newsstand. Finally we squeeze together in one last attempt. I hug everything she is to me and know it is not enough. There are so many promises and unfulfilled dreams lying between us. We are together until death.

"Good night, dear."

"Good night."

16

2

"Peter, come on, honey."

"I'm awake."

"I've got to get breakfast. You'd better hurry."

"Okay, I hear you."

The dark nest of bed. I can smell my breath bouncing off the bottom sheet. A smell of freshness passes in from the window. The sheets are always crisp and clean. A night's sleep cannot take their smoothness away. The bed is my wife's. All the furniture in the house is hers.

I push up and swing my feet to the floor. It is cold and oddly wet-feeling. My knees are stiff, the joints rocking bone to bone. Each night's sleep seems to take me closer to death. I return each morning from farther and farther away. I walk to the window and look out at the lawn. It is covered by a matting of leaves. The trees are color. The urge from my bladder pulls me to the bathroom. I can no longer make it through the night without getting up once or more. I hack phlegm into the toilet and wonder that it is I making this sound. I finish urinating and step to look in the mirror. The beard is heavy and rough. The mustache is dotted with perspiration.

"Daddy, can I come in?" My daughter outside my door, ready to give me my morning hug. I am amazed how she will come to meet me, while I must always chase my son.

"One second, honey."

I scamper back into the bedroom and pull a blanket off the bed. I drape it over myself and get down on all fours. I crawl to the door, the blanket nearly tripping me. I lean up and turn the knob. The door slides open slowly. She is standing in her pajamas, still closer to night than day.

"A bear!" she shrieks.

It is an old game between us. I lunge at her easily enough to allow her to escape. She darts down the hallway and I lumber after her. I smile when I see her duck into Ron's room. I roar louder. I can hear the laughter mixed with terror. As I round the corner, she climbs onto the bed. Ron looks at me and starts to smile but quickly hides it. He shakes his head wearily.

"Here he comes! Here he comes!" She is fighting to get under the covers. Ron clamps them around his body. He will not participate, but he will not allow the game to go on. I pretend to stand on my hind legs, sniffing the air. When I sniff in her direction, I growl ferociously.

"Let me in, Ron!"

I climb slowly on top of them, hoping for the nervous squirming to increase. Ron is stone. I growl louder and begin to maul them. Lori tucks her body beside Ron's, her eyes covered by pillows. I swat them firmly and roll my chest against their bed warmth. I wait to feel Ron's body slacken, but it is unbending. Lori is pushing me away with her hands.

"Stop it," Ron says. I growl louder. I am a whirlwind. I feel like the epitome of bearness. I want to cuff them into my arms and sleep for days. Ron's hands push frantically at my throat.

"Stop it!" he screams.

I lift off and see Ron's eyes. He is half-crying. He kicks his way from under the sheets and runs into the bathroom. Lori does not know how to take it. She looks to me to carry it off. I am as helpless as she is.

"Ron's afraid of bears," she says limply.

"I suppose he is."

"I'm not."

"Why'd you run then?"

"Because."

"Because why?"

"What else should you do?"

"To get away from a bear?"

"Yes."

"Get under the covers."

I pounce on her again. The game is over and we both know it. We are playing it out to have it finished. I have to shower and get ready. I have already forfeited my second cup of coffee.

"Scat," I say, and let her go. She runs off, giggling. I wrap the blanket around me and pad back to the bedroom. Morning sounds from the kitchen climb the stairs. I can hear my wife setting the table. It is a female rhythm. I cannot copy the sound to my own satisfaction.

"Are you almost ready?" my wife yells up.

"Almost."

"It's almost eight."

19

"All right."

I shower quickly. The water flows thick on my spine. There is never any point to stop in a shower. I get out only to have a cigarette. I rub myself dry and sort through my suits. They are conservative and drab. All my life I have worn earth shades. The sight of a sharp red or green offends me. A tall heel can make me question another man's integrity. A ring gripped in a handshake can undermine a business deal.

"Peter, it's eight-fifteen, what are you doing?"

My wife a whirl of motion in the bedroom. I try to move more quickly. I know deep inside it is her attempt to help me. She is the guardian of our welfare. It is her job to get me out of the house in time. Once I am out, I am on my own.

"Why are you dawdling?"

"Dawdling?"

The word plays over my tongue. It is a good word, a descriptive one. I think back, trying to remember the literature from college. There must be a word to describe a word that by its sound describes its own meaning. *Sludge* is the same. Sludge can only be sludge. But I know the meaning of *metaphor* and *simile* and *alliteration*; it is none of these.

"Yes, dawdling. Come on, honey."

I dress even more rapidly. I can feel the sweat already beginning under my arms. I want to tell her it is no use. I will never be big in business. I will never be a millionaire. Retirement will be a charade. We both know we will have to struggle to send our children to college.

"Is it nice out?" I ask.

"I think so. It's supposed to rain, though."

20

"Any sign of Plato?"

"No. I called for her this morning, but I haven't seen anything. I still think she's just wandered off."

"She couldn't have. How long have we had her?"

"You've had her. She was never really the family dog."

"All right. How long have I had her then?"

"Since Ron's second birthday. Something like that."

"Then how could she wander off? It would be easier for one of the kids to wander off."

"Oh, Peter."

Plato has been gone for three days. She was a gray black mutt with something like rickets. I fed her milk with soybeans. The kids pulled at her fur. She nipped one and was locked away in the basement, on and off, for close to a year. When she came out, she squinted at the sun.

"I'm sorry, honey." She moves closer to me. Her body is taut. It urges me to hurry, not to be late.

"The kids haven't even mentioned her, have they?"

"Peter, they have too."

"No, they haven't. They asked where she was, but they didn't care when I told them."

"What do you want them to do?"

"I don't know. The dog lived here their whole lives."

"It bit Ron."

"Ron was pulling her fur."

"Well, you can't blame him for being afraid of her."

"And you can't blame Plato for being afraid of him."

"Oh, Jesus, Peter, just come on. I have to get them dressed."

She is gone, her voice leading her down the hall. The kids snap to at the sound of her heels. They clatter down

21

the stairs, hungry and young. I tuck my tie into place and feel it jab against my Adam's apple. I swallow hard to loosen it. The watch is strapped on without thought. I dab after-shave on my collar and chin and place a drop beneath my nose. I will smell good to myself for at least the morning. When I hear their silverware scraping their plates, I hurry down. They are around the kitchen table, slurping cereal. The bright glare of the boxes pokes at me. Ron reads a box-top offer while he eats.

"Good morning, family."

Lori smiles, but the rest are too busy. I reach over Ron and pull the box away. I am aware that I am tormenting him. I am aware that he knows he is tormenting me. His eyes stab up at me, but I stare them down by dint of age.

"Three weeks to school," I goad.

The grapefruit in front of me has been rimmed and freed. The sections come out in the scoop of my spoon. I would like a bit of sugar, but it is forbidden. I bite into the strange, acidy taste and wait for the explosion on my palate. It is dulled by the morning flavor of toothpaste.

"So, what are you kids going to do today?" I ask.

"I'm going to Sally's," Lori tells me.

"Ron?"

"Nothing."

"Nothing? That could be tough. You're going to sit around all day?"

"You know," he says.

"Ron's going to clean out the basement for me, aren't you?" Jill intervenes.

"I guess."

"Good man."

22

I look at the dirty spot where Plato used to lie. It is next to the refrigerator, warm and safe. She liked the soft purr of electricity. At night, in the darkness, her eyes were two lighthouses.

"Peter, have you settled it with Charlie?"

"The house?"

"Yes."

"I told you, it's all settled. We can go up anytime in those two weeks. They won't be using it."

"Do you know where it is? I don't want to get lost in Maine."

"We won't. It's right off the coast. It's hard to get lost with the Atlantic Ocean to your right."

The coffee is warm and strong. The first sip goes directly to the bowels. I light a cigarette and watch the smoke drift out the window. The scotch from the night before is gone. The milky cereal laps to the motion of spoons. I check my body, looking for some weakness, some illness to let me stay home. I do not relish the hours in the office. I have glanced at the kitchen clock ten times already. A two-week vacation at the end of forty-odd workweeks. Christmas and Easter a struggle for extra days off.

"Charlie and Helen aren't using the house?" Jill asks, sitting down.

"They were up there half the summer. They go up on weekends. They drive half their weekends away."

"It's crazy."

"Yes and no."

"What do you mean, yes and no?"

"Just that. *Oui et non. Si y no.* No and yes."

Lori is laughing. I am magic with her. I continue the yes

and no until it is grating. I turn it into a song that fits loosely to the melody of "You say potatoes, I say potaaa-tooo." I make Al Jolson window-wiping motions. My wife gets up and pretends to be busy around the sink. Her sponge never stops. I have caught her wiping the handle to the refrigerator at midnight.

"You're goofy," Lori says.

Ron finishes his cereal and carries his bowl to the sink. It is rinsed and loaded into the dishwasher. I see him ready to explode. I am not sure if the distance between us is temporary. I search for psychological theories to explain it. The rejection of the father at a certain age is natural. He spins and walks off to the TV room. I wait until the sound of cartoons is loud enough, then call to him to turn it off. I can feel his moodiness as I light another cigarette. He slinks back into the kitchen and slumps into a chair.

"Sorry, Ron. No TV on a nice day like this."

"There's nothing to do."

"You can . . . you can get the tackle ready."

A change in mid-sentence. I cannot tell him to work. The tackle box has always been sacred. It has been off-limits to him. I see him lighten, his body fill with energy. It is a gift of time, of manhood to him. The tackle is ready now. I strain to think of a job for him to do.

"How about it?" I ask.

"What do you want me to do?"

"Clean the rods. Just wipe them down with a damp cloth. Go through the tackle box and make sure we have everything. You know that old gray box downstairs? The metal one? You can use that for your own until we can get

24

you a real one. You can take half the stuff for yourself. Set up your own tackle box. You can even have that penknife."

He is facing me now. His eyes are grateful, but I can see it pains him to show it. I want to run upstairs and change into blue jeans and a baggy sweat shirt and watch him organize his own tackle. I want to tell him the history of each lure, each fly. I want him to fill his box with my memories.

"What about the lures and stuff?" he asks.

"Take a couple."

"Which ones?"

"You can pick a couple. We can always trade back and forth, depending on what's working."

"I don't want the darter." He refuses my luckiest lure.

"Okay."

"You really mean it about the penknife?"

"Sure. Just be careful with it. My dad gave it to me."

"I don't want to lose it. Maybe I should wait."

"That's up to you. I always think things should be used."

"I guess so."

"What about me, Daddy?" Lori asks.

She is excluded. I can see Ron bridle. Jill moves in and sweeps away the plastic milk container. Her eyes wink at me.

"Aren't you going to help me, sweetheart?" she asks Lori.

"Do what?"

"Well, we have to sew some things, and I was hoping you would help me pack."

"Okay."

"I have to get going. Call me later," I say.

"All right, dear."

I kiss Lori lightly. I am afraid to kiss her on the mouth.

25

Ron sits quietly, timing my departure. I rub his hair and push his head back. His eyes are a mixture of sadness and excitement.

"I want to see a good tackle box, okay?"

"Okay. I'll clean the rods, too."

"Great. See you all later."

"Good-bye, honey."

A kiss from Jill. I spill out the door. The day is fine and clear. The leaves are glued to the grass. I can smell the richness of humus. I should be spreading seed for the coming spring. It is a winter away, but it must be thought of. To let the land go decreases its value. One must preserve appearances in order to sell them. I step into the garage and stop. The car smells of gas. The barbecue coals are dust. I walk slowly to the garage wall and lean against it. I place my ear to it, listening like a doctor to a heart. I can hear only the dull thud of my own blood pulsing in my temples.

3

People are milling about the office when I arrive. They are always reluctant to begin. I put my briefcase down and look for my coffee cup. It is plastic and cheap; a small mouse with a skimmer and cane dances on the side of it. I tell anyone who asks that my daughter gave it to me. They sigh and think how wonderful it all is. I don't tell them I use a cheap cup because all the others I have brought were stolen.

The coffee is industrial. It bites the back of the throat and falls apart. No one bothers to make it better than it must be. I stir in a white powder coffee helper that is outlawed at home. The wooden spoons are so many little oars. If one drinks slowly, he can wait until ten to begin work.

"Pete! What did you think of the Yankees yesterday?"

It is Charlie. I watch him approach and wonder at his large form, his quick, easy manner. He can talk in elevators. His lending me the house in Maine has drawn him closer. We are suddenly even thicker than before.

"They looked good," I tell him.

"Didn't they? They're going to catch Boston, I swear."

"Maybe."

"What's wrong with you? Bad weekend?" he asks.

"No, why? Do I look bad?"

"You just seem a little quiet."

"I'm not ready to start work. Sometimes I think they should let you do your forty hours whenever you want."

"Take it up with Alston."

"No, thanks."

"Just hang on till the end of the week. Then it's trout and the great outdoors."

"Why are they always called the great outdoors?"

"I don't know. Jesus, why are you always asking shit like that?"

"Like what?"

"Like all kinds of things. Remember that night we got drunk and you went on for an hour asking me why a chair is called a chair? You said it could just as easily be called a dog. You insisted that I pet a chair, just so you could prove a point. Jesus. We stopped talking like that in sixth grade."

"I do that?"

"Sure, but I like it. You get me thinking."

Charlie drinks coffee like beer. He swishes it in his mouth before swallowing. I can't imagine his coming from money. His parents are rich. They have lived to a grand age as if it were their right. Charlie is a son with three kids. His children are satellites around him. They have his mannerisms, his ease. He is a roast beef man with a cottage cheese wife.

"There he goes," I say blankly.

Mr. Alston crosses through to his office. His secretary hands him a sheaf of papers before he has shucked his coat.

28

It is the unofficial sign to begin. People peel away from the coffee machine. The eager are already at their desks, hoping for the eye to fall on them. I realize today I have nothing pressing to do. I duck past Charlie and fix another cup. It will be carried to my desk and placed there to measure the morning.

"Lunch?" Charlie asks.

"Sure. Where?"

"The Press. I want a sandwich."

"Okay. Come by and get me."

"See you later."

"Yep."

I go to my desk and rock into my chair. It is on swivels and sits on top of a plastic island. It creaks when I write. I slip out of my jacket and hang it across the back. I have nothing to occupy me. I pull out a newspaper and bend over it. Suddenly there is motion above me. I cover the paper like a school boy caught cheating. Lexi, the office mare, is in front of me. I try to look nonchalant, but her legs are too long. Her dress wags open just above the third button. I see a glimpse of silk before I catch her eyes.

"Good morning," she says.

"Hi, Lexi."

"Mr. Alston left these Friday. He wants you to look them over."

"Okay."

"No rush."

"I thought everything was rush."

It is a weak attempt. Her body hangs between business and conversation. Her mouth twists into a smile. She is

29

gauging me. In the office hierarchy I am her superior. I push back in my chair and take a sip of coffee. I want to hold her in front of me, to lock her in my gaze.

"Did you have a good weekend?" I ask.

"Okay. We went fishing. I've never been before, so you can imagine what I was like."

"Did you catch anything?"

"Some of those, what do you call them? Robins."

"Sea robins?"

"Yep."

"So you went salt-water fishing?"

"Yes. It was terrific."

"Did you get seasick?"

"No. I felt a little queasy when we started, but then it went away. Do you fish?"

"Yes. I'm going fishing next week."

"Vacation?"

"Yep. My two golden weeks. My small taste of retirement."

She laughs, to my surprise. Our eyes are not entirely innocent. I want to thank her, to kiss her for looking at me that way. It has been too many years since a glance meant anything. I have lost my way with women. I wonder if I have ever appealed to a woman as she appeals to me.

"Where?" she asks.

"Up in Maine. Charlie lent us his house."

I am not even aware that I have said "us." It is second nature. I see it register in her eyes, take the body, and reduce its slouch. We are once again on business terms.

"I didn't know Charlie had a house up there," she says.

"It's a camp. You know, no heating or anything."

30

"Well, it sounds like fun. I hope you have a great time."

"Thanks."

"I'll stop back for those papers later. Mr. Alston wants to see your comments."

"All right, I'll get on it."

Triangular calves flex away from under the skirt. Her hem strikes her knees and shows the hint of higher leg. There is a knot in my stomach that marks her leaving. A second form slips past her and moves toward my desk. Sally, a large woman with glasses dangling around her neck, smiles at me. It is the cautious smile of someone approaching for a reason. She is the head of the typing pool, a woman with strong, mannish fingers.

"I know what you think, and you're right." She laughs.

"What do I think?" I ask.

"You think I'm here to ask for money."

"Oh, come on, Sally. What is it this time?"

"They're carrying away another one of my girls."

"Who is?"

"Men! Who else?"

Sally has watched the long parade of brides type up their resignations. She has accepted them one by one in a tradition of loneliness. Her Frank, ever-present but dead fifteen years, spoiled her for other men. No one knows how or why. At each departure she collects a swarm of women around her nibbling at cakes and tea. When the cake is nearly finished, Sally produces a little shower present that has been picked by the congress of secretaries. She has memories of herself parked in a hundred homes around New York.

"Sally, I'm going broke. I might as well marry the girls myself."

31

"Oh, you! It's just a dollar."

"Who is it?" I reach for my wallet.

"Jennie, the new girl."

"I don't even know her, do I?"

"How should I know who you know? You sit at this desk so much it's a wonder you know anyone."

"Now don't yell at me while I'm giving you money. I won't take it."

"It's the truth. All you ever do is hang around with Charlie. There are a lot of wonderful people in the office if you'd only give them a chance."

"You make me out to be an ogre."

"When you give me the dollar, I'll take it all back."

"I'll give it to you."

"Thanks."

She slides the dollar into her fist. Her hand is lined and swollen. Her clothes are back in fashion without her even knowing it.

"How are Jill and the kids?" she asks.

"Fine."

"Don't you have a vacation coming up?"

"Yep. Starts this weekend. We're going fishing."

"Good for you. Where?"

"In Maine. Charlie's letting us use his place."

"Two weeks?"

"Yep."

"Well, you deserve it. Enjoy yourselves."

"When's the party?" I ask.

"What party?"

"The shower."

"Oh, I'd nearly forgotten. Friday afternoon. Be sure to come."

"Okay."

She resumes her prowling. I can't help wondering whether she herself contributes. I lean back and sip my coffee. The accounts Lexi handed me are dry and sure. I spin the figures in my mind, balancing them against estimates. It is all perfect. There are too many good minds working on it to find fault. I check again, knowing to catch something would be a coup in my favor. There is nothing. I have spent a half hour on nothing. I glance at the clock and see it is past 10:30. I am again without purpose. The coffee stirs my bowels enough to require relief. I look forward to the process each day. There is no one who can be criticized for going to the bathroom.

Henry and John are leaning against the sinks. The all-weather carpeting skids under my shoe soles. I nod to them and wonder what to say. John is a young man on the rise. He is already more valuable to the office than I am. He has a mind that grasps upward. He is a decision maker among sheep. Henry is the same age, but weaker. He is a plow horse. His clothes puff out in unexpected places. He is surprised at John's brilliance and dismayed at his own failings. They attended rival colleges and still carry it between them.

"Pete," John asks, "what do you think of the Hoffman account?"

"What do you mean?"

"Do you think we blew it?"

"Do you?"

"Maybe. I don't know. Henry says we handled it just right."

33

I cannot place the Hoffman account sufficiently for comment. It was not under my responsibility and therefore meaningless. I watch Henry, trying to decide how he has been defending his position. I want to support him, to give him a smell of blood from John's thick fur. But I know too little.

"I don't really know much about it. It seemed all right, what little I heard."

"See?" Henry asks.

"I still don't think so. But what the hell? We still draw wages, right?" John diminishes Henry's shaky victory.

I concentrate on the urinal in front of me. I hear them fade out of the room, their conversation continuing. They never run out of things to talk about. They are not so much younger than I, merely more hopeful. I turn away from the urinal and set the faucets running cold. I cup my hands and splash water into my eyes. I can't get enough. I want to swim down the pipes, to paddle out into the reservoir. As I bring the water to my face, I check my watch. It is almost eleven, an hour until lunch.

4

The Press is a thick guzzle of men and smoke. Old type-
writers line the walls. An old stage has been converted into
a raised dining platform. A few poorly tended plants sag in
greeting. The clutter of noise is a fair exchange for the
clutter in the streets. At the bar a row of men paw at their
beers and sandwiches. Every day the menu is written on
chalk boards six feet long. There is an old-time picture of a
naked woman reclining over the bar. It is the only picture
that could hang there. Behind the bar two hair-ringed men
pace back and forth. Their skulls glisten. There is little that
could be kicked and broken about the place. It is solid and
hard.

Charlie leads me to two seats at the end of the bar. We
take a certain pride in being regulars. Two beers are placed
in front of us before we can ask. Ben, the older one, wipes
the bar in front of us. He is a practiced bartender, a man
who has learned his trade from the movies. He snaps his
head back to indicate the menu. Charlie takes a drink of
beer and lights a cigarette. I search my pockets and remember I am out.

"What'll it be?" Ben asks.

"I'll have a roast beef sandwich," Charlie tells him.

"Make it two."

Ben goes off without a word. There are no questions about hard rolls or rye bread. There is no chance for extra mayo. Charlie bites into a green pepper and snorts smoke out his nostrils.

"Jesus, they're hot." he says.

"They're peppers."

"I know. I know."

"How did it go this morning?" I ask.

"The meeting? Fine. Same old bullshit."

"Always is."

"You're a cynical bastard today."

"Am I?"

"See?"

He takes another bite from the pepper. He swings it from the stem and gnaws at it sideways. I know without doubt that I love this man. I know that he is a slob at his job and he himself knows it. His own knowledge is more painful. He slumps a little on the barstool and squashes his cigarette. It smolders in the ashtray until he reaches over the bar and comes back with an ice cube. It sizzles once, then gives way to the coolness.

"Listen," he starts, "about the place. When do you think you'll go up?"

"This weekend."

"Saturday?"

"If it's okay."

"Of course it's okay. When you get up there, do me a

36

favor and look around the place. See if anyone's used it. The cops told me some teen-agers have been using it for the bangedy-bang."

"All right. Anything else?"

"No, I don't think so. I know I worry about the place too much. Sometimes it seems like the only worthwhile thing around, you know?"

"Yep."

"If it wasn't for the house and the Yankees—Jesus."

"I'll look around for you. I don't think we'll stay up there more than a week anyway."

"Suit yourself."

Sandwiches crawl halfway up Ben's arm. He unloads two to us and shuffles out four more. I open the top of the roll and spread the pickles out. The thick beef is red and stringy. It jams up to the gums on my first bite. The slow creaking of jaws around me is quieting. When I am finished with the first half, I want another. The press of my stomach against the bar ruins the taste. I take a drink of beer and feel it burn my tongue.

"How are the kids?" Charlie asks.

"Okay. Did Rich ever get stand-offish with you?"

"Why? Ron doing that?"

"Yep."

"Let me think. He's a little older, remember. I guess so. For a while there he didn't like to even be close. I could tell he was relieved when I went out to cut the lawn. You mean things like that?"

"Yeah. Does it go away?"

"Sure. Not all the way, though. You've got to remember

kids are people. Fighting to be people anyway. I think you always expect kids to be closer to you than they can be. Maybe that's an American myth. Don't worry. It isn't that they don't love you. They just want to be people and you can't be a person with a parent hanging around."

"Who's the cynic now?" I ask.

"That isn't cynical. It's true."

"Well, I hope Ron gets over it. I feel like a leper."

Charlie chokes on a mouthful of beer and meat. I can see the laugh churning his body. It is not particularly funny, but there is a need to laugh. He swallows with difficulty and the laugh persists.

"A leper? I've heard fathers think a lot of different things about themselves, but never a leper."

"Charlie, why don't you and Helen come up the second weekend? We can all drive back together."

"Up to Maine?"

"Why not?"

"No reason. I just hadn't thought about it. I figured you all wanted to be alone."

"We'll be alone all week. I don't know how much aloneness I can stand."

"I know what you mean."

"Well, see what Helen says. I think we'll be ready for some company."

"Maybe so."

Ben is back in front of us. He tells me there is a phone call and points to the back of the bar. I ask him who it is and he says it's my wife. I slip off the stool and walk to the phone. It is quieter there. The bathroms close by smell faintly of use.

38

"Hello? Jill?"

"Hi, Peter. Listen, I've got some bad news."

"What?"

"Ron found Plato."

"Where? Is she dead?"

"Yes."

"Where was she?"

"She was down in the basement."

"Where?"

"I've called the SPCA. They'll be right over."

"Where was she?"

"Oh, Peter. She was curled back behind the old bookcase. You can barely see her."

"How did Ron find her?"

"He . . . he smelled her."

"I'll be right home."

"Peter, I know how much she meant to you. I'm sorry. But the SPCA will be here, honey. You can't do anything."

"Don't let them take her. I'll be home."

The electric silence of the phone. The sounds of the bar are distant and strange. I walk back to Charlie and tell him the news. He takes it straight, swiping a pickle from my plate as we talk.

"Tell Alston I won't be back today," I say.

"What should I tell him?"

"I don't care. Tell him anything."

"All right. I'll call if there's any problem."

"There already is."

"You know what I mean."

The bar peels off me. It is odd to find it day outside. Clouds are bunching to the north. Forty minutes from now

I will be back in suburbia. I will bend into a corner and whisper to Plato.

The driveway is covered by a thin film of water. I watch the trees blow a second before opening the car door. The oil in the blacktop shines blue. I see Jill waiting with the screen door pushed open. Her face is worried. For a moment she seems the Irish mother watching her sons give their lives to the sea. I try to name the play and the author, but it has been too many years. When I climb up the steps, she pushes back to let me in. The kitchen is warm and stuffy. A large pot bubbles on the stove. I can smell beef stewing away its cheapness.

I am stuck into a role, a cameo. I roll my shoulders to feel the morning settle. I am the homecomer, the meat gatherer. If I relax for a second, I will lose it.

"Where is she?" I ask.

"The SPCA was here. I told them you wanted to see her first. They said they'd be back."

"I'll bury her."

"Oh, Peter, I know how much she meant to you, but you can't do that. There must be ordinances and everything."

"I'll bury her."

"You can't. Come on, Peter, try to relax."

The basement door is a vault entrance. I push it open and find no smell of rot. I turn quickly and throw my raincoat on the chair. It hangs limp, the smell of the outdoors still clinging to the sleeves. I start down the stairs and stop midway.

"Where are the kids?"

"They're out."

"They don't give a fuck, do they?"

"Peter, stop it!"

I switch on the bare bulb and feel grit under my shoes. The basement is rough and sturdy. I cross to the bookcase and look into the corner. There is nothing there. I look again and see the dark shape of Plato. She is curled into a ball, her tail almost circling her head. I can smell her now, rich and true. I don't know how to go on. With an effort I reach along the bookcase and pet her. The fur is thickly matted. There is no answering quiver.

I stand up and open the door to the garage. At the top of the stairs I find the old blanket we use to rake leaves. I pull it down and drag it into the basement. A leaf slides dryly to to the floor.

"Come on, girl," I whisper.

I am glad we are alone. I reach back and search for a purchase. I lock on her front leg and give a tug. She is stuck, her body bloated with death. I pull harder and hear a slight crackling sound. Her back legs are unbending, the bones brittle and small. I pull her again and feel the smell pack into my nostrils. It is the death smell, though I've never known it before. Her muzzle pokes into the hard light and I see it is covered with vomit. Her teeth are bared in a snarl. I can see she went in pain. For a moment I wonder if she's been poisoned. Her eyes are half-closed in an addict's nod. Something scurries away behind the bookcase, but it is only motion. I cannot bring myself to look.

"Here, honey," I say.

41

I drag her onto the blanket and curl it over her. I feel better seeing her on the rough wool. As I try to drag her on completely, the back legs drag the blanket with them. I let go and walk around back. Her anus is covered in yellow. The blanket tucks over her like a diaper.

She is heavy in my arms. I carry her out the door leading to the garage. The air is fresh and wet. I wonder if I should change into jeans, but the SPCA will be here soon. I could not hand her to them. There is no sense in owning property if you cannot bury your own dog. Tucking her under one arm, I pull a shovel off the wall. It is a sharp spade used to chip ice. The grass licks my pants cuffs. I set her down next to a flower bed and turn the first spade of dirt. It is clean and heavy. It rolls in front of the spade like ice cream spilling in a wave on top of itself. I gain a slow rhythm and lose myself to it. My hands ache quietly. I hear footsteps behind me, but I can't stop.

"Can I help, Peter?"—my wife with her arms crossed. Her hair blows in the wind. She has a small sweater wrapped around her. I want to swear or cry, but she is too kind.

"How about making some coffee?"

"Is that all? Are you sure?"

"Yep."

She is a scythe going back to the house. I lift a worm out on the end of the blade and throw it near a bush. I don't want to think of worms. Straddling the hole, I lift Plato over it. My arms work like an arcade crane. I lower her as best I can, then drop her into the hole. Her body makes no sound. I try to think of something to say, to do, but nothing comes to mind. I reach down and cover her eyes with the corner of the blanket. The first shovel of dirt rattles free of

42

the body. I cover her lightly, end to end. Finally I push the dirt on hard and fast. She is gone quickly. There is only a brown patch of newly turned earth to mark ten years of friendship. I will wait until spring and plant a tree on top of her so that the roots can feed on her eyes.

5

The Piscataqua bends underneath us in a torrent. It is high
or low tide; a time of lather. A tugboat groans from Ports-
mouth, and we leave New Hampshire behind us. A sign a
mile farther along tells us we are welcome in Maine. The
pines wave behind it, and here and there a tree of color
flashes its plumage. There is a feel to Maine that is unlike
anywhere else. It is rough and slightly savage. Stone walls
dip off until they are replaced by the stone walls of the sea.
I-95 stretches straight into the greenery. I look in the rear-
view mirror and see my children napping. Lori's head lags
toward Ron's shoulder. My wife studies the countryside,
gathering details to be told and retold. She sees more than
I do. I have followed the Yankee game on radio until Hart-
ford. In Worcester I picked up the Red Sox.

"How do you feel? Tired?" she asks.

Jill rubs my neck. It is a secret warmth between us.
There are nights that I fall asleep with her hand tangled in
my mane. I push my head back against her fingers and feel
a chill run down my spine. I try to imagine her sitting close
to me, her hand locked on my thigh. It has been too long;

there have been too many clear rear-view mirrors in between. She is a door leaner now.

"I'm okay. It isn't much farther," I say.

"What exit did Charlie say?"

"Ogunquit. He says Ogunquit is a fairy beach."

"Homosexuals?"

"Yep."

"Why did you call them fairies? That isn't like you."

"I guess I have less tolerance these days."

"Why?"

"I don't know. Maybe taxes."

"Come off it."

"To tell you the truth, I don't know why. I heard myself laughing at a 'nigger' joke the other day. I felt sick when I did it, but I laughed anyway. I didn't do that before, did I?"

"Nope. You were a stern voice of social consciousness."

She reaches over and gooses me. She giggles nervously. I am not sure how I am going to be toward her this vacation. There is a pressure to perform. Already I am calculating how many days are left. Two weeks are fourteen days. Two days of driving leaves twelve. A day before we leave we will have to pack. Jill will scour the house for Helen. That leaves eleven at best. Two of the days will be halved in search of groceries. Other things will undoubtedly crop up. We will be lucky to have eight uninterrupted days. It seems too long and too short all at once.

"When are Charlie and Helen coming up?" she asks.

"Next weekend. You're sure you don't mind?"

"Positive. It'll be fun. Do you want to stay the second week?"

"Let's wait and see, okay?"

"Okay."

Jim Rice has hit a rope against the left-field wall. I try to listen, but there is static now. The woods on either side of the road are deepening. It is hard to picture the ocean lying off to our right. I remember dreams of living in a cabin in the north woods. I can still dream it at night if I push my mind hard. I know that the house in suburbia was never a dream. It was the sum of an equation. I cannot picture it unless it is in my sight. It has no form, no shape. The water for it comes from a reservoir I never heard of.

"Is that the exit?" she asks.

"Yep."

"Where do we go from here?"

"Up Route One a little ways. There's a Mobile station we take a left at. Then we follow that road for ten or twelve miles. At the end of it there's a dirt road, and the third house is it."

"Easy."

"It's supposed to be."

I veer the car off toward the toll booth. A man in a mackinaw collects my money. We follow the signs to Route 1, then head north. The Mobile station is where it should be. My wife rolls down her window and hangs her head out. She is still a pretty woman. I look at her thighs and ass as they press toward me. There is no stirring inside, no rise at all.

"God! I can smell the sea! Can you smell it? I think it's the sea!" she says.

Ahead of us the dirt road laps out. It is a brown tongue in a green backdrop. I ease the car onto it and listen to the shocks. Ron wakes up groggily and sucks a string of drool from his shoulder.

"Where are we?" he asks.

"We're there. Lori," Jill says, "wake up. We're here."

The car rattles over the bumps as we count the houses. They are set back among the pines. They look cheap and totally without foundations. There is an occasional glimpse of the lake to jog us on. I look back and see Ron's eyes lighting. Lori is squirming in her seat, afraid Ron will see something before she does. There is no one around. The birds dance from branch to branch.

"There it is! There it is!" Ron screams.

"Where? Where, Daddy?" Lori asks.

I stop the car and wonder where to park it. There is no driveway, only a small dent of pine needles. I move the car into the slot and turn off the engine. The silence is over-whelming. The land still rushes up at me. Ron is already out the door and darting toward the lake. Lori runs awkwardly behind him, shouting that it doesn't matter who is first. Jill walks around the hood of the car and smiles at me. The pine needles under my feet feel too real to be believable.

"Oh, God, it's beautiful!" Jill says. "Isn't it something? No wonder Charlie loves the place."

"It's nice."

"Nice? Peter, relax! Can't you enjoy this?"

She is slightly angry. She is right. I run toward a pine tree and embrace it. I kiss the bark and begin humping it. She laughs wildly and begins throwing pine needles at me. They slide down my shirt, but I can't stop. She runs up behind me and squeezes me against the tree. It rises a mile

47

above us. I turn quickly and judo-trip her to the ground. She falls softly, my body on top of hers.

"You're nuts." She laughs.

"I love you."

The words are too solemn, but they are good to say. I kiss her deeply and feel her body soften. She pulls me tight and whispers in my ear. I kiss her again and again. My fingers dig deeply into the forest floor.

"Daddy! Ron splashed me! Daddy!"

Unloading the car is pure drudgery. I feel the weight of a mobile household with each load. There are toys in case the kids get tired of a hundred acres of lakes and forest. There are make-up kits and thick best sellers. I balance each armful and waddle to the house. I climb three steps onto a porch and stop again to look at the lake. It is almost as blue as the chlorine oceans in the backyards at home. I want to be out of my pants and shirt. I want to feel the cold grip of water around my ankles.

The rooms inside are spartan and clean. One room has four bunks lined against the wall. Charlie has shown me pictures of it all before. The pictures showed me nothing about the feel of the place. It is a hunter's cabin, prime and hound-lazy. A potbellied stove stands pregnant in the sitting room.

"Where do you want all this?" I ask.

I give up responsibility as soon as the baggage is inside. Jill steps out of the kitchen and tells me to put it in a chair. I dump it quickly and walk out for more. My eyes cannot stop looking at the lake. There is a rocky shoreline and a small pier. Ron is skimming rocks and Lori is mimicking him. Ron gets two jumps. I know I can get three with the good flat rocks.

"Honey, why don't we leave all this for later?" Jill is standing next to me.

"It'll be dark."

"No, it won't. Let's take the kids in for a swim. I could use one, too."

There is no need to convince me further. I whistle to the kids and tell them to come inside. They climb up the small bank, eager as dogs. Jill roots out their bathing suits and hands them out. There is a moment of embarrassment because there are only two bedrooms.

"Come on, Ron, we'll get dressed in here," I say.

He follows me meekly into the bunk room. It has been a year or two since I've seen him naked. I find myself wanting to see his narrow body. I strip off my shirt and ignore his look. My chest seems absurdly hairy. I wonder what my penis will look like to him. I step out of my pants and make no move to hide myself. His own body is covered in a thin sheen of sweat. I see his small buttocks and want to cup them in my palms. He is without sin, without a blemish. He wriggles into his tiny trunks and wraps a towel around his neck. My movements seem old and smooth by comparison.

"Ready?" I ask.

"Yep."

He leads me out onto the porch. His legs flex at the knees and bundle in small knots of muscle. I cannot keep my hand from falling on his shoulder. He lets it rest for a polite moment, then moves away. We turn and see the two girls coming out. Lori is already hen-stepping. I make a horse sound and swing her on my back. Her thighs are silk around my hips. Jill looks thick through the buttocks, but there is still the woman sway to her walk.

"Let's go," I say.

We walk as a family to the water. The trees are thick on both sides. Charlie's house is tucked back into a small inlet. There is a sandy beach a couple of yards wide. I look at the rocks and see slugs clinging to them. I know this lake is filled with fish.

"Let me down." Lori is angry. Ron could easily be the first one in, but I see a moment of doubt cross his face. He is a suburban boy in a wilderness. It pains me to see his fright and ignorance.

"Come on. We'll all go in together," Jill says.

The water is numbing. I feel my anklebone turn brittle and stiff. There is a silty bottom giving way gradually to sand. I move one foot in front of the other to act as a minesweeper. Lori shivers and clamps a hand on her crotch. Her little shoulders could shake apart. When I am up to my knees, I realize the kids are already in to their waists. I push on more quickly. Suddenly I am trapped by a need to be immersed. I feel dirty, soiled. I fall forward and splash down to the bottom. My head aches from the cold. My testicles curl up to my body. I open my eyes and see the brown, translucent water stretch out in all directions. I pull myself along by my hands. I finally surface, breaking water like a whale. They all are jumping up and down. Lori is wet, but her head is still dry. Ron is splashing Jill and she is pretending to be angry. I swim back toward them like an alligator. My eyes are the only things visible. Lori screams and

giggles at the same time. Ron paddles softly away. Jill backs
up and begins splashing at me.

"Don't you dare! Stop it, Peter! Don't! Don't!"

I grab her around the knees and press forward with my
shoulder. She falls heavily, the water too shallow to support
her weight. When I raise my head, I see she is sitting as if in
a bath. Her body is wet only from the waist down. She
shakes her head and laughs. I look to see Lori is disap-
pointed that the attack was not for her. I make an elephant
trumpet sound and begin pushing toward her. Her arms
whack at her sides in excitement. Her lips are blue. The little bathing suit straps fall from her shoulders. Her teeth
clatter and a thick vein stands out on her temple. "Daddy!"
she squeals.

I grab her thin legs and know that I can do anything with
her. There is no weight, only a snapping motion. I lift her
over my arm and begin to count. She has her hands wrapped
around my neck.

"O---n---e." I rock her.

She is screaming. Jill tells me to be careful. I say,
"T---w---o!" Ron is paddling by himself. Lori is frantic. She
has a vivid imagination. Suddenly she is no longer laughing.
She is starting to cry, her arms a vise around my neck.

"No, Daddy! Daddy! Daddieeeeee!"

I let her down in my arms. She is not sure she didn't want
to be thrown. I wrestle her slowly into the water and she is
happy again. We are a family of otters, sunning ourselves in
the last swell of autumn. Something deep stirs inside me.
It is a need for redemption, for a second baptism. I realize
I am twenty feet out toward the center of the lake. I am

surrounded by water. I don't remember leaving my family. I swim breaststroke, enjoying the water slithering over me. I want to slip out of my trunks and feel the cold press on my rectum. I switch onto my back and look up at the sun. It is sharp and clear against the horizon. I feel a cleanliness coming back to me. There is a superior order making a mockery of my own attempts at order. I want nothing more than to live in the rhythm of the days.

6

The porch is a twilight between two worlds. The sun glows heavily across the water. I sip a lukewarm beer and smell dinner cooking. Jill is planning spaghetti with sauce out of a jar. She has found everything to set the table. She has made a careful list of condiments and cans so we can replenish anything we use.

The mosquitoes are large and insistent. I take another sip of beer, then pull my sweater over my head. I have the clean feeling that only swimming can give. My hair is wet. A trickle of water falls into my ear and temporarily deafens me. Ron and Lori are collecting shells. They are still trembling with excitement. I lean back in the rocker and try to calm myself. The slow pace now permissible is lost on me. I am unused to sitting and watching a day end.

"Look, Dad."

Lori holds up something from the shore and I wave back. I have no idea what it is. Seeing the lake and trees before me is causing a dull throb somewhere inside. My life is out of control. I am trapped into waiting and needing more than is necessary. I remember my father sitting at the head of the kitchen table. We were grown then, all of us with ambitions of our own. My mother was dead, a victim of restlessness. She did not understand it when her last child had gone off to college. She did not understand that she was no longer needed. And my father was alone. That night we passed him presents and watched his eyes. It was Father's Day. He had been retired for more than a year. Each of our presents was geared to give him something to do. My sister gave him a bird feeder and a field guide to identify the birds when they came. Another sister gave him a splicer to edit the spotty home movies he had taken of us growing up. The gifts were expensive and well thought out. They had taken more time to choose than anything we had ever given him. But it was obvious to everyone that they were designed to fill the void we left. He opened each more slowly than the one before it. His fingers trembled on the ribbons. When he was finished we sang "Happy Father's Day" to the tune of "Happy Birthday." He smiled, thin and weak. A few nights later I stopped in and found him paging through the field guide. It was dark out. I pretended to have forgotten something in my car and ran out, crying into the darkness.

"Can I join you?"

Jill is dressed in casual clothes. Her hair is swept up in a bun. A glass of ice and scotch jangles in her hand. She sinks into a wicker chair and sighs. She looks out at the deepening night and smiles. I want to crawl next to her and ask if she is happy. I want to be her for a moment, to know all she is thinking. The two children below us passed through her body. She is richer for it, more stable. I have never created anything.

"God, it really is beautiful," she says.

54

"Yep."

"Do you think you could live like this? I mean all year round?"

"I think so."

"I don't know if I could. I'd like to think I could, but I'm not sure."

"Why not?"

"Well, I might get bored. It's peaceful, but there isn't much to do. Maybe I could. I don't know."

"What would you have done if we hadn't gotten married?"

It's an old question between us, but its purpose never changes. I want to know I haven't cheated her.

"Jeeez, who knows? I guess I would have gotten married somewhere along the line. I never wanted to do anything too spectacular. I guess I would have liked the thought of ending up like this even then. You know what I mean?"

"I think so," I say.

"You're different, though, aren't you? You always wanted to do something special. What did you call it? Large! Everything was large or small to you. Do you remember? This was a large book, this was a small film. You hated suburbia then, too. You thought anyone who lived in suburbia was small and doomed. Remember that poem you made up? How did it go? Something like:

> Sam the sad salmon
> spawns all day long
> he cuts up his lawn
> and withers his dong.

That's it!"

She roars with laughter. I can't fight the smile that works its way onto my lips. She is right. She stands and walks into the house. There is sauce to check. I am back to myself and the fading sun. It is strange not to have the bleat of a radio or television. The crickets are beginning. Out in the lake a few trout make feeding rushes and break the surface. I think I see them glint for a moment before they dive back down. Ron and Lori look like two animals drinking their fill for the night. I try to think of a way to sneak up on them, but I am too comfortable. I sip the beer again and find I have finished it. I want another, but I'm afraid to lose the edge of hunger.

"Peter, could you call the kids?"

I relay the message and watch them come toward me. When they reach the light of the porch, they are once again my children. I tell them to knock the sand off their feet. Lori lifts her leg back and away, already female.

"Daddy, it's neat! I think we saw fish. Didn't we, Ron?"

"I think so."

I see he is beginning to thaw. The possibilities of the lake are too vast for him. I stand and feel the beer go to my head. I have lost my drinking ability long ago. There was a time I could open my throat and drink as fast as the liquid could come forward.

"What do you think, Ron? Any fish?" I ask.

"Yep."

"Which lure are you going to use?"

"I don't know. What are you going to use?"

"Well, until we get a boat, I was thinking of just using slugs. It wouldn't really matter what we caught."

"Come on, you all," Jill yells from the kitchen.

We move inside. The table is completely set. Except for the obvious differences, there is no distinguishing this meal from a thousand at home. Jill will not serve until all hands are washed. Without the TV there is no rush to have it over.

"Where are we going to sleep?" Lori asks.

Jill fills her plate with spaghetti. The store-bought sauce is thin.

"You both can sleep in the bunk room," Jill says.

"With him!" Lori holds her nose and points at Ron. It is all a farce. She is crazy about the idea.

"Can I sleep outside?" he asks.

"Maybe later on," I tell him.

The noodles are hard for them to handle. Jill cuts the pile on Lori's plate into forkfuls. There is a silent understanding that Lori is Jill's responsibility, Ron is mine. We push the sauce around our plates with whole wheat bread. There are no empty calories for these children. Dessert is administered like a prescription.

The meal unwinds. It is getting cold. I go out to the sitting room and close the door. I am reluctant to do it. With the door closed we could be anywhere.

"What are we going to do after dinner?" Ron asks.

"What would you like to do?"

"I don't know. Can I go out?"

"It'll be pretty cold. You won't be able to see in the dark."

"Yes, I can."

"Why don't we read a story?" Jill says.

"Which one?" Lori asks.

Jill has seen this coming. She rattles off a list of stories suitable for children. Lori is pulling for the classics she knows by heart. Ron is aloof. I wonder at my wife's ability

57

to predict. For years she lived in a child's world. Even now she can impersonate cartoon characters that the children recognize immediately.

"I want to read *Charlotte's Web*," Lori says.

"Ron?" Jill asks.

"I don't care."

"I'll tell you what. Let's make a deal with the womenfolk. If they'll read the story and leave us to getting the tackle ready for tomorrow, we'll build them a fire."

Lori squeals. I know I am being hokey, but I can't help it. It is not fair to draw these sex distinctions, only convenient. Ron weighs the idea. He cannot help admitting it is a good one. Jills smiles at me secretly.

"Okay," Ron agrees.

We push away from the table. Lori reminds Jill that we have no marshmallows. Jill says she will fix up something. I don't know how, but I don't bother to ask. Ron follows me out the door. It is full night. Without streetlights and buildings it is incredibly dark. I see Ron slow. He has forgotten his desire to come out by himself. At the woodpile he is afraid to touch the logs. I pick them up and hand them to him. He holds out his arms until they are full. Suddenly he screams and drops them.

"There was something on them," he says, trembling. "A spider or something."

"It's okay. Okay."

His fear is swelling. I want to tell him there is nothing to be afraid of. His fear passes through me. I question whether he could pick up a tadpole or garter snake. There are things one must learn as a boy to know.

"You don't have to carry any if you don't want to," I say.

"I will. It was just a spider or something."

I am careful not to load him too full. As soon as he can, he darts off into the house. I can't tell what it is that scares me so much about him. I see too much of myself in his small frame.

I pause for a moment and look out at the lake. It is choppy now, the water pulling at the shore. I seem to hear a wedge of geese above me. I don't know if they can fly at night, but I know warblers can navigate by the stars. It is a deep season. It creeps inside and stirs forever. A tremendous yearning dances in on me. I want to rock back on my haunches and howl. Little makes more sense to me than the cry of a coyote. I know I have let too many seasons pass unnoticed to demand payment from this one, this moment.

I climb the stairs and open the door. There is a drawing-room warmth to the scene. Ron has piled the kindling next to the stove. I drop the heavier logs on top and begin making the fire. Jill has mashed the tiny marshmallows she uses in fruit salad into lumps. She tells Lori that we will spread them on graham crackers and make "some-mores." I hate her for her efficiency. She embroiders the world of childhood while I stammer on the edges.

"Ron, want to make the fire?" I ask.

"I don't know how."

"It's easy. Come on, I'll show you."

I show him how to roll the newspapers to get maximum warmth. Under my instruction he builds a tent over the kindling. It is stacked so the air can get through. I check the vents for a third time and tell him to light it. It crackles and wells to life. I am surprised at my own ability. The arts of the male were passed down to me in bits and pieces. The rest is logic and patience.

"There you go, Ron," Jill supports him.

"Good. Now, when that burns down, lay on the next size logs. Don't try to speed it up. Let it get good and hot," I say.

We should chase them into pajamas, but it is chilly. Jill sits close to the fire and begins reading. The pig in the story settles the mood around us. It is a country story, just right for this cabin. I am worried about the spider's upsetting Ron, but it comes and goes without a ripple. I tell him to get the tackle boxes. He goes off to a closet and comes back with both. He is embarrassed by his own. It looks small and ugly next to mine. I would give him mine if it would change their appearance.

"Let me see," I say.

"I just took a little."

He has hardly taken anything. His dull gray box is almost empty. I know he is afraid to take from me. I ladle out line and hooks. I give him one or two lures he knows I love. His box fills quickly. We fit together our poles and put the reels on. The creak of the line going out punctuates Jill's reading. When it is all the way through, we tie on the leaders. I tell him we can use bobbers the first day. Lori is getting restless, watching us. Jill senses it and puts down her book.

"How about some marshmallows? Come on, Lori, you can help me."

Jill holds a long fork over the flames. Lori watches intently. I can feel Ron straining to join them. I can't release him. I know I should put down my tackle and help Jill, but I am selfish. She pulls out a brown glob of marshmallow and spreads it on a graham cracker. Lori gets first bites. I wonder at the practical knowledge so easily handed down from woman to woman. I have nothing to show Ron day to day. He suddenly seems like a lump of clay I can't quite throw. He spins in front of me, my foot pumping the pedal. I reach out and touch him and see his character shaped. It spins faster in my hands until the clay is too thin. I stop, afraid that I will crumple him. But the pot is unfinished and poorly thrown. I want to melt him down, begin again. Instead, he keeps spinning, the centrifugal force pulling him farther and farther apart.

"You guys ready?" Jill asks.

"Go ahead, Ron, have one."

He sets down the tackle too carefully. His movements are measured. Jill hands him the fork with the marshmallow already wadded on it. He pokes it into the flames. Lori watches him, her fingers caked with white. I glance at my watch and see it is almost bedtime. One day is already gone.

"Good, Ron," Jill says.

"That looks yummy," Lori plays the little girl.

He spreads the gunk onto a graham cracker. Jill pours a little chocolate syrup on top. Ron holds the whole thing between two fingers. It trembles in his hand. He turns to me and holds it out. I don't know what to do. I reach out and take it, my eyes locked on his. I have never received such a gift. Jill watches, her eyes moist. I can see Lori fidgeting, slightly jealous. But it is Ron's moment, complete and solid. I bite into the marshmallow and roll my eyes. It is a forgotten taste. Ron laughs. It is the sound of a fever breaking.

"God," I say, "oh, God."

"Good?" Jill asks.

"Delicious. Now you have one, Ron. Thank you. It's delicious."

I watch them cook for another half hour. Lori's lips are turned into a clown's. Ron works with a steady hand. Jill picks up *Charlotte's Web* and continues reading. They are at the fair. Charlotte is writing "What a Pig" in her web. I gaze at the fire and listen to the trout night hunting in black water.

7

I feel the morning long before waking to it. It comes as a restlessness, a call. I open my eyes and see it is still dark. I have the alarm set, but it isn't needed. The floor beneath my feet feels foreign. It is north-country cold. I breathe deeply and smell the pine resin. It has been years since such a morning. I slip into the sitting room and climb into clothes. The slightest sound seems out of place. I am afraid it will disturb the coming light; crack it like a double yolk into a black iron skillet.

I open the door of the cabin and walk out onto the porch. There is a struggle of light. Something close to the water runs into the underbrush. It was surprisingly large, surprisingly alive. I suck yards of air into my lungs. I half think I could quit smoking on such a day. There is a pleasant wetness on everything. I am reluctant to go back inside, afraid to miss what is happening in front of me. Activity obscures, strangles the quality of real sight.

I pad back in and open the door to the bunk room. It smells of children. Ron is on the top bunk and I shake him softly. He wakes and I help him down. He shivers off the bed warmth and walks quickly to the sitting room.

"Hungry?" I whisper.

"No. You?"

"I'm going to fix some coffee. No, no, I won't. Let's get outside."

I watch him dress. It is incredible to me that he will dress each morning for the next fifty years. I try to picture him old, but it is impossible.

"Put on the waders," I tell him.

We both slip on the waders. His are small, borrowed from Charlie's boy, Rich. The rubbery sound is entirely a man's. His excitement is growing. I hope for him to have the first fish.

"Set?" I ask.

"Yep."

"Let's go."

We clomp into the front yard, carrying our tackle boxes, poles dangling in front. I am happy to see it is no closer to daylight. When we get to the beach, we set the equipment down on a rock. Ron looks to me for instructions. I lead him to the large boulders and begin picking slugs. Their secretion is slimy and wetter than the lake. When we each have enough, we go back to the poles.

"Easy, huh?" I ask.

"Yeah."

We wade into the water. It is ice-cold for a moment. There is a liquid feel to our legs despite the waders. I am slowly growing conscious of the lake. There are pops of feeding fish and ripples of movement. It is total gray. I almost slip once and remind Ron to be careful. I stop when he is to his hips.

"What looks good to you?" I ask.

"Over there, by the rocks."

"Probably so. Why don't you start there, and I'll cast out toward the center?"

"Okay."

He moves away on heavy legs. I have not noticed until now how small he looks. I see him fight to bait his hook. He is awkward and the pole is too big. I start toward him, then see he has made it. He slides the pole back and lets the first cast go. It plunks in the water twenty feet toward the rocks. I force my eyes to let him go.

The slug oozes black blood as I hook it. The cast brings back a hundred memories. It is the motion of something ancient and true. It separates me from the world, then ties me back to it in the right way. I prop the pole in my armpit and fight a cigarette out of my pocket. The sun is pushing its way into the morning. I can barely feel the house behind me. The cigarette ashes sting the water. I am slowly caught up in the fishing. I reel in the line and cast again. There is no need to be in the water. We could sit on the rocks and cast once. But it is the feel of it that's important: the motion and the stillness.

I hear Ron scramble and see him almost lose his balance. The rocks underneath are covered with moss, or lichen, or whatever grows. He says beneath his breath that he had a nibble. His voice carries across the water and rushes by me. I rack my mind and try to remember having a game of catch with my father. He was too old. We are always too old for our children, but his was a full age. I think back, trying to remember some advice he gave me, some philosophy. There was nothing. He was full of advice like "Don't drink and leave your money on the bar" or "Don't ever write anything to a woman you don't mean to live up to," but that was all. There were no guidelines, no attempt to push me beyond his own limits. I was a success in his eyes before he died. I was no better or worse than his own reflection.

"Dad!"

His line quivers. He is tied to the life of the lake. I see the water break and the fish jumping. It is not the jump of a game fish, only the throes of a deadening madness. Ron is pulling hard. The click of the rod is sharp and metallic. The fish is closer to the rocks than it should be. It could tangle there, get enough leverage to break free. Ron can think of nothing but speed. He reels faster and faster until his hand is a blur. The fish is being towed, not played. When it is a few feet in front of him, the line goes slack. He throws a look at me, but I can't explain. Suddenly it begins pulling again. The fish has been resting, examining the two green pillars of legs. Ron swings him free of the lake and the fish gasps. It is making a crying sound, a harsh suck of air that will never be enough. It is large. The rod bends like a bow. Ron does not know what to do. I walk quickly to him and grab the fish. It is still crying. I would like to tell him what kind of fish it is, but I have no idea. It is slick in my hand, its skin the color of the lake.

"What do we do with it?" he asks.

"Eat it," I say.

"I mean now. What do we do?"

"We have to kill it."

"How?"

"Hit it on the head."

"How?"

"Carry it to one of the rocks and knock it on the head." He can't believe me. Killing is a lesson that must be taught. We wade to the rocks and take the fish off the line. It is still now, paralyzed for air. I remind myself not to make light of this. It is a first greeting from death.

"What now?" Ron asks.

"Do you want to kill it?"

"I guess."

"Do you understand that we're going to eat it? And that it's better to kill it than let it suffer?"

"Yes."

"Don't ever just kill something, Ron. It doesn't make sense. Everything in nature makes sense except that. You're part of that, you know? After you've killed something, you become even more a part of it."

"Okay."

I don't know if I am making it more morbid than it needs to be. It is a fish, nothing more. I decide to kill this fish for him, then decide against it. I want him to know something of death.

"Just hit its head against the rock," I tell him.

"Slam it?"

"Hit it hard enough. Do it once right."

He pulls his arm back and taps the fish on the rock. The fish nearly squirms out of his hand. I nod and tell him to do it again. He cranks and slams it hard. A trickle of blood spills from its mouth. Ron sticks it under the water and shakes it. I can't tell what he is doing. Perhaps he is trying to revive it.

"Now pull one of those little branches off the bank and put it through the gills. Leave it in the water so it'll stay fresh. Okay?"

"All right."

I wade back to my position. I glance to see him threading the branch through the gills. The sun is on us. It weaves through the earth sky and presses on the lake. It is a day almost too clean for killing. I suspect if someone kills a great deal, he can learn something of life. I cast again. The one fish has put an end to the fishing. I don't care anymore. I light another cigarette and look around. There are no houses except Charlie's. It is a virgin lake.

"Hello!"

It is a man's voice. He is dressed as a fisherman. I did not see him approach. He is suddenly there, on the bank, as if he jumped out of a tree.

"Hi," I answer.

"Get anything?" he asks.

"Ron has." I point.

"Using slugs?"

"Yep."

"Where's Charlie?"

"At home. He lent us the place."

"Oh. I live right next door. My name's Mark Clutier."

"I'm Peter and this is Ron."

"Hello again."

"Do you live up here? Permanently?"

"No. Just like Charlie. I get out of Boston on weekends. I drag my wife along to cook what I catch."

The man is brisk. He is no stranger to the woods. He squats on the bank with the ease of a cowboy. I do not know how to proceed. I wouldn't mind the company, but I also want to be alone. The man decides for me. He pulls his line to him and spears a slug. He slides noiselessly into the water. He is my age, my build. But he seems more alive, to have more blood.

"Beautiful morning, isn't it? Do you mind if I fish with you?" he asks.

"Not at all. You can probably show us a thing or two."

"Fishing's luck, that's all. The more equipment I buy, the fewer fish I catch."

"That's the way, isn't it?"

He spins off a perfect cast. His movements are relaxed and sure. I see Ron edge farther away. I can smell the man over the lake. He is shaved and cologned. His belly is flat and solid.

"Hate to fish alone," he says.

"It can get boring."

"You from New York?"

"New Jersey. I work in New York."

"I never cared much for New York. Boston's getting just as bad. Seems this is the only place I enjoy."

"Do you come up often?"

"Like I said, mostly on weekends. Some people buy these places as an investment. I bought my place because I found I was spending a lot of weekends mowing the lawn. God, it's pitiful when you work all week and there's nothing to look forward to but mowing the lawn."

"I know what you mean."

He casts again. He is workman-perfect in all he does. His

accent is rich and strict New England. I want to ask him to say "park" and "yard." Ron tries a cast, but it gets tangled around his pole.

"Nice-looking boy," he says.

"Thanks."

"Any other children?"

"A little girl, Lori. How about you?"

"None. Wish I did. I could give you a long explanation, but the simple fact is we don't have any kids. Leaves a lot of loose ends."

"What do you mean?"

"Well, it just seems like kids are the only point to anything. I don't love my job. It's okay, I like it, but I don't love it. I don't know anyone who loves his job, but I know a lot of people who love their kids. You know what I mean?"

"Sure."

"Fishing always gets me started. Ask Charlie. I can't keep quiet."

"I enjoy it."

But I don't enjoy it. He seems an invader, a harsh break in the morning's silence. I have had too many words for too long. I have had to say the right thing too often. Behind me the house is coming to life. It is only dawn, but there is something to get up for. I try to think of ways to fend this man off. He is the boy in fifth grade who always borrowed my notepaper, just to speak a word. I move a little farther off. I am hoping the lake will divide us.

"What are you in?" he asks.

"Business?"

"Yes."

"Accounting."

"I'm in banking. Pretty much the same thing, huh? Dull work."

"It can be."

"Well, it pays the rent. That's half the game, isn't it? Making ends meet isn't very interesting, but without it, what would we do all day?"

"You've got a point."

His line darts forward, slicing the water like a scalpel. He nods to himself and begins playing the fish. He is masterful. His wrists flex and toss the fish about. He cares nothing about catching it. It is the cat and mouse he enjoys; the exhaustion of a lesser species. I know without question his house is a model of design and efficiency. He is a gimmick man, a lover of dials and malleable metals. He carries flares in the trunk of his car.

The fish rolls on its side close enough to touch. He reaches forward and frees it. It is a casual gesture. The fish can't swim. He reaches down and herds it forward. It swims away a few feet, then rolls back on its side.

"It's dead," he says.

He tries to pick the fish up, but it squirms away. It can't right itself, begins paddling in a circle. It stops intermittently, gills pulsing. The one eye I can see is a disk of wonder. There is no blinking to quiet it. It is a beam of accusation. Mark tries for it again, and again the fish flops forward. It swims around and around, running from death but getting nowhere. Mark finally gives up. The fish rests, seeming to sense its safety. It cannot do anything to save itself.

"Strange, huh?" he asks.

"Yeah."

71

"I don't want to leave him like that, but what the hell?"

The sun is full on top of us. I can smell food on the wind. I want Jill to call us in. I tell myself I will cast once more. It is a subtle form of gambling I have long played with myself. I always grant myself a last chance. "Good morning."

Jill is calling from the bank. Her arms are hugged to herself. She is younger than the night before. Her cheeks are red and healthy. I reel in my line. Ron yells that he has already caught one. I know I am taking too long in introducing Mark, but I can't help it. I am unable to break the silence.

"You all ready for breakfast?" she asks.

"This is Mark, honey. Jill, my wife. Would you like to join us for breakfast?"

"No, thanks. I should be getting back myself. Why don't you all stop over for a drink tonight?"

"We have the kids and all . . ."

"Bring them. Or, if you'd rather, we'll bring a bottle and have a drink over here."

Jill can hear only a little of this. It is my decision anyway. She doesn't know him. I try to think of a graceful way out, but there isn't one.

"Okay. Around eight?" I say.

"Fine."

"See you later then."

"All right."

I pull slowly out of the lake. Ron runs onto the bank, holding his fish in front of him. Jill smiles and they laugh that I haven't caught anything. When we are completely out of the water, I listen for the fish flapping in a circle. But it is quiet now, warm and quiet.

72

8

We climb into the car, the clean clothes stiff on our limbs. We are a hunting expedition. We are searching for food and toilet articles; we sell the comfort of the day for another comfort. Ron's fish is clean and gutted. I can feel the beach-like sandiness in the toe of each shoe. The woods peel away slowly. Ron is annoyed at having to leave. He has been on the lake like a dragonfly. Lori is already bored. I would gladly give this afternoon if it were to be the last. But I know there will be more trips, more needs.

"We can just go right up there." Jill points ahead.

"Where?"

"Right there."

"Where, damn it! I don't see it!"

"Peter, stop yelling. It's right there."

I follow the line of her finger and see the sign for the supermarket. It was obscured but still visible to the calm eye. I turn on the blinker and cross the line of oncoming traffic. Cars spin around the mouth of the store. A big-breasted woman in a halter top stares through the wind-shield. I can't name the anger inside me. It is more than the waste of a day. It is the uselessness of buying and consumption. It is responsibility. We are wasteful and excessive. Each trip is tagged with the demand for a toy.

"Everyone ready?" I say.

"Can I stay here?" Ron asks.

"No," I tell him, "come with us."

"Why?"

"Just come. Lori, take your mother's hand."

The dictator leading his small battalion into the store. The electric eye whisks the doors open and closed. There is the smell of purchase. A book rack squeaks to the vibration of the air conditioner. The odor of fresh vegetables mixes with the stench of detergents. It is more than sterile. The boxes are lined in disgusting order. Cellophane covers everything. Two fat women waddle in front of us, calculators hanging from their wrists. It is the ultimate barter, the appetite rendered into a computer.

"Can I push it, Mom?" Lori asks.

"Why don't you both push it?"

"Forget it," Ron says.

Lori goes on her toes and leans against the cart. It rocks forward and drags her down the aisle. Dead music is playing over the PA. It occurs to me that we are being anesthetized. Jill begins loading the cart with a practiced motion. She picks through lettuce and produce with the movements of a native in an open-air market. I light a cigarette and try to take an interest. I remember going with my mother on long shopping trips. On the way home I would climb into the back seat and fall asleep. More than once I woke to the sepulchral darkness of our garage, the car long still, the packages all put away.

"What do you feel like having this week?" Jill asks me.

"Anything."

"You said you wanted to get some lobsters. What day do you want to have them?"

"I don't care."

"Come on, Peter." She is exasperated.

"I don't care. May God strike me dead if I care."

"You'll complain later on."

"No, I won't."

"Yes, you will. You always do."

"I do not."

"Peter, I'm going to ask again. What would you like to have this week?"

"Moose meat."

"Come on." Her voice is a whine.

I hold my fingers behind my head and dance around the aisle. Lori and Ron giggle. I watch Jill's face closely, hoping for a smile. There is also a part of me hoping she will scream. Lori puts her fingers behind her head and wiggles them. Jill yanks the cart away from her and walks away, smoldering. I know it is no use to go after her. My imitation of a moose was noncooperative. We can be anything, but first of all we must be a team.

I walk to the wine rack and look at the bottles. I can speak French but know nothing of wines. Jill has swept around the corner to the meat section. Ron and Lori are stranded between us.

"Why don't you guys help me pick out some wine?" I ask them.

They walk toward me, happy to have a direction to take. Lori wants the prettiest bottles. Ron tries to show some

75

judgment, but he can't take himself seriously. I pick out two whites and one red and carry them to the cart. Jill does not look at us. She is bending over the meat, inspecting the prices.

"Find any moose meat?" I ask.

She turns to me. Her face is flushed. A plastic-wrapped steak glistens in her hand. I see her flare for a moment, then subside. The look now is deadly and cold. She flips the meat sideways and it lands with a flop on the floor. "Fuck you, Peter," she whispers.

She walks off quietly. I can feel the violence trailing after her. Lori begins to follow her, but I call her back. I bend and pick up the meat.

"Why did Ma do that?" Lori asks.

"She's angry."

"Why?"

"Because I was being a jerk. Fathers can be jerks."

"Why, though? Why were you a jerk?"

"Shhh. Come on, we'll finish the shopping. Okay? Who can find me a package of chicken breasts? It's right over there. See if you can pick it out."

They scatter over the meat counter. I can't be angry at Jill or myself. I am too numb, too tired. I do not love or hate her or expect anything from her. Jill's anger will pass. Everything will pass, including me. There is only the next step that demands attention. There is only a bowl of stew to prepare, a finger of gin.

"Which kind do you want, Dad?" Ron asks.

"The boneless kind, I think. Better get those."

"What are we having?" Lori whines.

"Chicken and barley."

"I hate that. Can't we barbecue?" Lori asks.

"Not tonight. We will one of these nights."

"When?" Lori wants to know.

"I don't know."

"That means we won't," Ron tells Lori.

"What does?" I ask.

"When you say you don't know, it means we're not going to."

"Yes, we will. Just not tonight."

"We don't have a barbecue," Lori says.

"So? We can make a campfire."

"Neat."

"Can we, Dad?" Ron asks.

"Of course? Am I Simon Legree?"

"Who?"

"Never mind."

"What do we need next?" Lori asks.

"Bread and butter."

They run off in a version of a scavenger hunt. I wheel the cart along serenely. Not one person I pass is less than ten pounds overweight. A gray-haired man stamps prices on fruit cocktail. He nudges them onto the shelf and bends for more. I think of Jill and know she is out in the car. She is wondering how to come back inside, how to mend the fabric of a placid day. We do not normally allow such scenes. It is too true, too alive. We are better than honest emotion. We are civilized to tedium.

The kids return with their arms full. I send them off for more. I can't be bothered with comparison shopping. I want to be gone. The woods are a hope. I can feel young for a moment when my skin is clean.

"Let's go. We'll get the rest tomorrow," I tell them.

"There's still some stuff on the list," Ron says.

"Tomorrow."

"Okay."

The check-out counters are dipping pens. We plunge into them, struggling past the rows and rows of candies. I can no longer feel sorry for the meat I eat.

"I'm sorry," I whisper across the seat.

"How could you do that?" Jill asks.

"I'm sorry, I'm sorry. I know it was stupid. I'm sorry."

The engine ignites in the silence. She knows I am not sorry and she doesn't care. It will pass because it must. In five minutes the car is back under the pines. I carry the packages into the house. I offer to unload them, but she takes over. It is early evening. I realize the sun drops quicker than it rises. We will have to get ready for Mark and his wife. We will have to make ice. The ice will freeze the smiles on our faces. One more drink, one more night of babble, one more deadened sleep.

"How about a swim, you guys?" I yell.

"Yeah!"

"Hurry up then."

I change into my suit and wait. I turn from the kitchen and go back into the bedroom. A manila folder is wrinkled with neglect. I pick it up and tuck it beneath my shirt. The kids are ready on the porch. I run out and chase them down the hill. Ron throws off his shirt and plows straight in. Lori picks daintily at the edge, then gives a squeal and falls in six inches of water. She is all teeth and smiles. I pick her up and wade in. Ron porpoises in front of us.

"Just a quick dip. Hurry up," I say, ducking down.

They flail at the water. It is not wet enough for them. They cannot get enough of the splashing and quiet underneath. When I tell them to get out, they giggle and shout. Jill is clanging pots, trying to reach me.

"Okay, that's it."

"Ah, Dad." Ron sighs.

"Come on. Out."

They march up and the chill takes them. They hurry inside to heavy clothes. I stand in the sun and let the water fall. The sun is on a level with my eyes. It leans against a pine and hangs there winking. I dry my hands quickly on my shirt and pick up the folder. I remember buying it, the quick exchange of money over the dime-store counter. I called it by a hundred different names. It was the workbook, the scrap heap, or simply the folder. It held twenty or thirty poems. In the rush of youth I was to be a poet, a writer. I spent long nights scribbling at the paper, stuffing the folder to the breaking point. It was a private dream.

I open it slowly. Even in its age I recognize the first poem. I read it line by line, then stop at the end of the first stanza. I back up onto the rocks and sit. I begin again.

> The bat
> precision flight,
> angled to the wings
> fly hunting, hair tangling,
> black shadow of night.

I turn to the next. It is the same. It is an eruption of words, a short statement of self-consciousness. Poem after poem is the same. A distant part of my mind asks why I brought them with me. They are dead. I wonder that I thought I could write. It is belittling to read old words. On the last page I find a strange poem. It is nothing like the others.

> Sam the sad salmon
> spawns all day long
> he cuts up his lawn
> and withers his dong.
> When mad men or night
> stalkers get in his
> way, he takes back his
> office and cuts off
> their pay.
> But who pays Sam the
> sad salmon and who
> explains why he swims
> up the river and gets
> home just to die?

There is even a date under it. I lived in a dream of its becoming valuable one day. The early scratchings of a genius. But now it is painful and ludicrous. I am forced to see my youth was absurd. Even my dreams were lifeless. I ask myself again why I brought them. I thumb back and forth, looking for an answer. Suddenly I begin to cry. It has no purpose. Still, I make no attempt to stop. I bend over and tuck my head on my knees. I shiver from my testicles. I wait for the surge of self-assurance, of rationalization, but nothing comes. It is a long weeping. I finally jump back in the water and swim furiously out into the lake. I cannot give a reason to stop. I roll on my back and look up. There is nothing in the sky. There is, quite simply, nothing.

9

A dot of light moves through the trees close to the lake. I reach up and make sure the collar of my shirt is stiff and straight. Jill cannot sit down. It is acute torture to her to have two strangers coming for drinks. There is so much to calculate, so much to primp. She has been wondering all evening what she can offer them in the way of tidbits. I tell her it doesn't matter. Our peace is newly penned and freshly inked. A quick kiss sealed a healthy confrontation. We are back to shadowboxing.

"Hello," Mark calls.

He holds up a bottle and snags the footpath with his flashlight. His wife walks behind him, her hand in his. Jill darts back inside for the finishing touches. She will mold her hair with deft fingertips. She will carry out a bucket of ice and try to act casual. Oh, hello, she will say, as if our lives were made up of evening drinks at poolside.

"Pete, this is my wife, Roxana." Mark spins his wife toward me.

"Hello, Pete."

"Hi. Have a seat. My wife will be right out."

Roxana is more than I expected. Her clothes are bright but trimly cut. A tight scarf tied gypsy-fashion covers her head. Two bangle earrings drip down either side of her neck. Her eyes are deep-set and wandering. She is long-tapered; there is a cigarlike quality of grace and smoothness to her. Jill seems to bound onto the porch by contrast. She holds out a hand to them both, then sinks into a chair. She knows at a glance she is outmatched. Roxana is liquid in her conquering.

"Mark tells me you're from New York?" Roxana asks.

"New Jersey actually. What will you have?" I ask.

"Scotch," she says.

"Same," Mark nods.

"Four scotches then."

I move to the card table bar and mix drinks. Roxana is following me with questions. She adores New York. She loves its excitement. Jill makes an excuse and darts back inside. I hand out the drinks and sit back down.

"New York is really like anyplace else," she is saying, "except that it is magnified. It's as if the gravity or density changes, and people and events are suddenly three times as heavy as ordinary events."

"Ah, New York. You can have it," Mark says.

"But it's the center of so many things. I was raised just outside the city, in Fort Lee. It changes you, growing up near it. It may sound odd, but I've never felt comfortable with anyone who hasn't spent some time there."

"I haven't, and you married me," Mark snorts.

I laugh just enough. The drink is all I want right now. I

83

light a cigarette and then think to offer them to the others. Mark waves them away, but Roxana takes one between long fingers.

"I only smoke when I drink." She takes a light.

Jill hustles out with cheese and crackers. It is too cold on the porch, but I can't invite them inside. I want to feel them close to leaving. I wonder for a moment if Roxana is making a play. Mark keeps her in check with little love pats. He is more nervous than I thought. His forearms have a mechanic's bulge.

"Are you from New Jersey?" she asks Jill.

"No, I'm from Baltimore."

"Is Baltimore as ugly as they say?"

"Well, I don't know. How ugly do they say it is?"

The ice is broken. Roxana coils back, though she laughs harder than anyone. Jill passes hors d'oeuvres. She is ashamed of the Ritz crackers we lap up with soup. The scotch is rising in me. I can feel it reach my fingers and start back. I know if I get a moment alone, I will take a swig from the bottle.

"Where are the kids?" Mark asks.

"They're getting ready for bed," Jill answers. "Ron is exhausted."

"I told your husband. He's a handsome boy."

"Thank you."

"I think I'd worry about them being a little isolated if they had to stay up here all the time, but it sure is great for them to have this time," Jill tells us.

Roxana takes this in. I can't tell if she is a refined person on her way down or a gum snapper on a social mountain climb. I want to turn the conversation toward literature. I want to recite books and ideas in a monotone of knowledge. We are all pulling in our own directions. The podium is passed with the crackers.

"How far is it to Boston?" Jill asks.

"About an hour and a half," Mark says.

I know I could ask him how many miles he gets to the gallon and he would tell me. He is sure to change the tire pressure with each contemplated trip.

"Before I forget," Mark continues, "we have a canoe. You're more than welcome to use it this week. I've got it locked to the little pier in front of our place."

"Well, we were going to rent one," I say.

"Nonsense. I don't use it enough as it is. Don't be silly."

"It's awfully nice of you."

"Not at all."

"Mark always tries to talk me into going fishing with him. I can't stand it. I've never seen the attraction. It's so God-awfully boring," Roxana says.

She finishes this last bit with too much self-awareness. She is losing us more and more each time she talks. She is a theatergoer and a charity worker. I fix more drinks. The mosquitoes are exposed nerves in the ears. The lake rocks in its bed. Suddenly the door is pushed open and Ron and Lori file out. The light from inside reminds us it is full darkness. Mark sits up in his chair and shakes hands with both of them. Roxana makes an offhand comment about the purity of children in pajamas. She is womb-empty. All that is good about my wife is lost on her.

"We've only a cat," Roxana says.

Jill runs the kids inside. It occurs to me that our house could run without me. I have no job here. Mark begins telling me about the good fishing spots around the lake. I sit back and slosh the scotch. I can look out through my eyes and see myself as others must. I am a type. I am a home builder and a milk provider. I have no great faults and no great assets. If my hair is not combed in exactly the same way, day after day, my scalp feels violated.

Roxana is getting sulky. She is already deep into the scotch. She could drink more quickly, but I make her wait. It is a growing effort to be polite. I know Jill is spending more time inside than necessary. I find myself liking Mark. He is a hundred ways I am not. He is clockwork in a haphazard world. I would want him as a neighbor. I could buy him beer and let him tinker with my car. If the lawn mower broke, I could give him an afternoon of enjoyment. He needs no payment but what his hands can give him.

"Well, that's over." Jill is back.

"It's a full-time job, huh?" Mark asks.

"Full-time isn't the word."

"Would you want to work when they are old enough?" Roxana asks.

It is an obvious trap. Any way Jill responds will be an opening for Roxana. I want to take Roxana and run her hands over my children. I want to make her bend and smell their breath. This is work, I would tell her.

"I haven't given it much thought," Jill says.

"It must be tough seeing them go off, though."

"It's not as if they join the Foreign Legion at ten."

"No, I didn't mean it that way. I just meant as their needs decrease, yours increase."

Jill is annoyed. She is no good at words. She takes a long drink and lets the ice rattle. Roxana takes another

86

cigarette from my pack. I light it and tuck the dead match in my pocket. A wind falls on the lake and sets it rippling. I think of the manila folder stretched out on the sand. I offer it to the wind, pray the wind will take it. I don't want the embarrassment of the past. I scoff at young people's ideas and call them Pablum. I have grown gut-proud in my knowledge of the way the world ticks. I have too sharp an eye for reality. I have too high a regard for facts.

"Who wants another?" I ask.

"Okay," Mark says, "that's the nice thing about walking. You can drink as much as you like."

"Me, too." Roxana holds up her glass.

I wait for Jill, but it is not her night. She will throw her sober weight on us all. She will be sharp and miss the humor of the dullness. I pour more into my glass than the other's. It is a challenge I set for myself. I want to see how drunk I can become and still act normal.

"Jesus, you think that fish is still paddling around in a circle?" Mark laughs.

"It might be."

"What's that?" Jill asks.

"I caught this fish and tried to let it go. But it must have lost its equilibrium or something because it couldn't get straight up and down. It paddled around and around because it couldn't use both fins."

"Now Mark will tell us the allegory," Roxana says.

"What?" he asks.

"Go ahead." She turns to us, her hands moving on her lap like a woman doing needlepoint. "Mark sees everything in allegory. Especially nature. The fish going around and around is, let's see, Man? It must be Man because Man is always going around and around. He has some marvelous ones. He's not satisfied to use the normal ones. It's all very inventive."

"I do get carried away sometimes," Mark admits.

The *sometimes* is an afterthought. He knows she is attacking him, but he can't defend himself. I feel sorry for him because I am the same way. It is a way of piecing together information. I take a sip of scotch and find the glass is almost empty. Jill is cringing. She yawns from nervousness and the conversation closes like a rose.

"Well, we've had our drink," Mark says.

"Listen, take your bottle. We haven't even cracked it."

"No, keep it. It's annoying to have to run downtown all the time."

"We have plenty."

"No, keep it. I'll drink it anyway, next time Charlie's up."

There is a small laugh to send them off. He clicks on his flashlight and the beam is incredibly strong. It is a flashlight for a man who lives in readiness, who lives for disaster. They weave slightly as they go toward the beach.

"Oh, stop over for the key tomorrow. For the canoe," Mark says.

"When are you all leaving?" I ask.

"Around noon. Stop by anytime."

"Okay."

Jill shivers as soon as it is safe. We both are considering ways to begin the nastiness. I know that fifteen minutes from now we will have them analyzed. We will shuffle them between us and square the deck.

"Want a drink?" I ask.

"A short one."

"Is it too cold out here?"

"No, I like it."

"What did you think?"

"Of them?"

"Yep."

"I'd say you should hide under the bed until after noon."

"That bad, huh?"

"Do you intend to work after they go off to school? We have a cat, don't you know?"

It is a fair enough imitation of Roxana. Jill sighs and puts her feet up on the chair. I want to pull a chair next to the fire inside and fall asleep with my head on my chest. My tongue is thick. My drinking has increased, when I drink, in these last years. I have learned to use alcohol as a corridor to sleep.

"Mark's nice enough," I say.

"Yeah, he is. But she's the kind of neurotic that I hate."

"Why?"

"She's so soooo. She wouldn't admit to watching TV, but she probably knows every character on the soaps."

"So?"

"Sooooo."

I cannot get as excited as I should. This is fresh, blue-stamped beef. Jill is ready with her knife. I am only numb. I hand her a drink and mark the coating on my gums. The thought that we are being attacked in the next house adds no fuel. I am tired of words. I have long ago misplaced the newness of people.

"She was an ass," I say.

"She liked your ass."

"Come off it."

89

"She did. Didn't you see her?"

"See what?"

"The whole thing. She was oozing it. If you had mentioned lunch, she would have handed you a matchbook with the name of the restaurant."

The wind is picking up. I begin to calculate how many days are left, but I stop as quickly as I start. I think it is possible that Roxana would have tumbled. I have had only one affair since I've married. It was short and sweaty. The woman and I broke off after a long procrastination. She has never called since. Our sex was warm and married. Only the clothes and restaurants were different.

"I'm going in," I say.

"Me, too. Let's leave this stuff until tomorrow."

"Fine."

"Are you fishing tomorrow?"

"Yep."

"Are you going to get the canoe?"

"Why not? It would be fun."

"They really weren't so bad, were they? I'm just getting old."

"No you're not. You're still a vixen."

"Ha!"

I bend over her and kiss her thin neck. My toes play from side to side to keep balance. I feel her warm. Her breasts are familiar weights. The old perfection and imperfections of her skin no longer surprise me. I know the pattern of her pores. When her hands begin to roam, I stand back. I try to think of a quip that will show her I am only slightly in the mood. She does not pursue. She stands and grabs an armful of clutter. There is a quick sound of water in the sink, then

90

a deeper one from the bathroom. I know she will be tucked in bed when I get there. I will crawl into the small tent of blankets and press my body against hers. We will roll until we find the right position. Night after night we sleep front to back. One upon the other, we sleep like spoons.

10

Again the morning. One sniff and I know the threat of rain. Birds call cautiously, branch to branch. I walk to the porch window and look out. The sky is still dark, but there are flecks of motion. The lake is rearing. I glance down at the porch and see crackers strewn over the dull wood planks. We have had a night visitor. I try to identify the animal by its treatment of cocktail crackers. We have no animals in the suburbs. A crowlike bird flaps down and picks at the crumbs. Its feathers are black electric. A gust of wind surprises it into flight. It circles over the beach and lands in a tree. It watches the porch for danger. The pines rustle the coming of autumn. A thin chip of cheese blows into the grass.

"Dad?"

"Hi, Ron. It's going to rain."

"Can we fish?"

"No, I don't think so. It wouldn't be worth it. It's going to rain soon."

"Can't we fish until then?"

"It's going to rain pretty soon."

"What if it doesn't?"

"Come here." I ignore him. "Look at this."

"What is it?"

"Come here and look."

He looks out the window and opens his mouth. I stifle the impulse to scare him with bear stories. I have decided it was a raccoon.

"What was it?" he asks.

"I don't know. Probably a raccoon."

"How big do raccoons get?"

"Not too big. They're smart, though."

"Could we shoot it?"

"Why would you want to shoot it?"

"I don't know."

"Maybe it was just the wind. I'll tell you what. Why don't we get dressed and go out and see? Maybe there'll be some tracks. We can get some wood, too, and then cook breakfast."

"Okay."

He pulls on his clothes. His legs make a sweet sound against the denim. He swings a sweater over his head. He needs no time to gather change and cigarettes. He is comfortable with his pockets empty.

"Ready?"

"Yep."

The wind presses against the door. It is the freshest day yet. The dirt is moist in its waiting. There is a season stirring that is undeniable. Winter is making its first advance. Calmness and panic are interwoven. Ron straightens the card table and looks around. Winter death is foreign to him. He is too sure of his own survival.

"Think there are any tracks, Dad?"

"I don't know."

"I think those are some."

"Where?"

"Right there, by the steps."

The prints are of human hands. They are tiny and dry. It is obviously a raccoon.

"There'll be tracks by the water, too. Raccoons have to dunk all their food before they eat it," I say.

"Why?"

"I think it has something to do with their saliva glands. They don't have enough saliva to swallow right."

"So they dunk everything?"

"That's what they say."

"Neat."

"Raccoons use their hands a lot. Actually they use their paws, but their paws have amazing dexterity."

"What's dexterity?"

"They can use their hands like humans. Their fingers can grab stuff that most animals can't. They even fish with their fingers."

"What do you mean?"

"They eat crayfish. You know, those things that look like lobsters? They feel along a bank, and when they feel crayfish, they pull them out."

"Are you kidding?"

"No, I'm serious."

"Could we do that?"

"I suppose. They can pinch, though."

"What else do raccoons do?"

"Let's see. I think their babies are called cubs. In the old days people used to hunt coons with dogs. They still do in the South, I guess. The dogs tree the coon and then the hunter gets it. Sometimes it doesn't work, though. Sometimes the coon gets away and sometimes they actually drown some dogs."

"How?"

"They lure it into the water; then they climb on its back."

Ron is satisfied. We walk over to the woodpile and he loads his own. He is less afraid than before. I am happy with my lecture. I have a thousand things to tell him about animals. I have watched "Wild Kingdom" for countless Sunday nights. I know the bear does not truly hibernate. I know a bighorn sheep can spy a crouching mountain lion at half a mile or more. I want to mention more to draw him on. It is not often I can fit my life to his.

We carry the wood into the house. He hovers in front of the stove, waiting to hear if I want him to make the fire. I tell him to go ahead. He smiles and begins rolling newspapers. I go back outside and drag the card table in. I toss the cheese and crackers onto the grass. The porch is empty except for a dilapidated rocker which puffs back and forth like a sail. I close the door behind me, and it is the first time it feels good to have the day beyond the door. It is satisfying to know there is noplace to go. I stand by the window and watch the storm build. Warmth is warmth only when there is cold to compare it to.

"Hungry?" I ask.

"A little."

"I'm going to start breakfast. Think you can get the fire going?"

"I think so."

"Just do it slowly."

"Okay."

I go into the kitchen, my boots sounding fine against the wooden floor. I turn the flame on under the frypan. It is a morning to have the smell of bacon. I am careful not to jingle the silverware in the drawer. My mind dims to the slow motion and easy thoughts. The bacon leaks onto the pan. I turn the flame down to keep the grease from spattering. I scoop coffee into the pot and add the prescribed amount of water. I catch the light from the window as the clouds catch it. The bacon pulls slowly apart. I divide it easily and look in on Ron. He is struggling with the fire. I can see it flicker for a moment in his eyes.

"Got it?" I ask.

"Almost."

We are gradually becoming a team. I wonder if I'm showing enough attention to Lori. She seems too perfect to need help. I wonder for a moment if all parents love one child more than another. The bacon snaps me back. It is drifting through the house. My wife and child will wake to the smell of bacon, coffee, and a wood fire. It is a rare gift. I get a paper napkin ready for the bacon. We are a greaseless family. Eggs are drained and cholesterol is counted. We will live a hundred years of caution.

"How is it going?" I ask Ron again.

"Okay. It's started."

"Well, if you can leave it alone, how about setting the table?"

"All right."

He follows me into the kitchen and I hand him the plates. There is juice for the kids. I have the rhythm now and the meal is coming together. I know it is selfish to wake the sleeping on a day like this. Ron bangs a plate on the table and looks to me for a reprimand. I roll my eyes. I think of Plato, dead almost a week. Her body is hot with decay.

"Good morning! Isn't this something! The two of you cooking breakfast."

Jill is standing in the doorway. Her hair is pulled back in the way that makes her forehead shiny. The old cardigan she stole from her brother is wrapped loosely around her. The tuck of her pubic area is sharp and clean.

"Hi, honey."

"No fishing?"

"It's going to rain."

"Well, we can just relax and enjoy it. I love a good rainstorm."

"We had a raccoon last night. Dad and I saw the tracks," Ron says.

"Did you?"

"It ate the crackers you left out there."

"It's a cultured raccoon, no doubt."

"Dad says they can fish with their fingers. Is that true?"

"If your dad says so."

It is odd to hear me referred to as Dad. I have never grown used to it. Jill comes to the stove and squeezes my bicep. It means a number of things. She checks the coffee and puts some odds and ends on the table. Ron goes out to check the fire.

"I'll get Lori up," she says.

"No, I'll get her. Will you watch this for a minute?"

"Sure."

I stop to look at the fire. It is going perfectly. Ron lays a

97

piece of wood on top and strains to hear a comment. I tell him it is fine and open the door to Lori. She is curled in a ball, her knees almost to her chin. The air snatches at the curtains. I sit on the edge of the bed and watch her. I am afraid of my love for her. I know I will try to protect her and expose Ron. It is wrong, but I can't help it. She is more woman at her age than Ron is man at his. It will be a fight to let her grow up.

"Lori. Loriii."

I brush her hair away from her forehead. My teeth are clenched from love, from the fragility that she is. I could cup her skull from ear to ear with my palm. She wakes slowly. Her hands stretch out, searching for the blanket. I grab one and squeeze it. When we walk hand in hand, she holds two of my fingers. I remind myself to be pleased when she takes a man to her bed.

"Good morning, sweetheart."

"Good morning, Daddy."

"Sleep okay?"

"Yep. What are you doing?"

"Waking you up. Hungry?"

"Yes."

"Well, if you hurry, there might be something left."

"I will."

"But first you have to hug me. I won't be able to save you any bacon if you don't!"

"Okay."

She hugs me around the neck. I tell her to hold on. I stand and feel her body swing against mine. She is smaller than a grocery bag to carry. I pretend to slip on something and act as if I'm falling. She squeals but giggles, too. I do it again and she laughs in my face. Her breath is not clean any longer.

"Okay, hurry." I set her down.

"All right."

"Ask Ron about the raccoon."

"What raccoon?"

"Ask him."

The bacon is in a crisp pile in the kitchen. The eggs are bubbling around the edges. Ron is at the table drinking juice. Jill is once again in charge.

"Is she coming?"

"She'll be right here."

"Let's eat then. Come on, Lori," she calls.

Lori runs in, half-dressed. Her hair is tangled and strange from sleep. She is comical but lovely. She rifles questions at Ron and gulps juice. Jill sets the food on the table. I wait for the others to go, then help myself. The rain begins on the roof and drips through the mesh of the screen. I can hear the wind circling, looking for a way in.

I look around me and see a scene out of a women's magazine. The day has sealed us off. The fire is no longer morning-strong. It is a necessity now, a warm coal-pan in an unheated bed. Jill sits tucked under an afghan, sewing with unnerving concentration. Ron and Lori paint or draw, their pencils rivaling the scratching of the branches. I cannot read my book. The lines waver and snake off the page. They are only so many words. There was a time when I lived for the well-turned phrase. Now it seems only pretense and foolishness. I want to challenge the whole family to a game of Monopoly, but I know what it will be like. Ron will whine when he can't win. Lori will be eaten alive.

"What time is it, Jill?" I ask.

"Nine-thirty."

"Is that all?"

"You were up at five-thirty. It just seems like it should be later."

"I think I'll run over and get the key."

"What key?" Ron asks.

"Just a key."

"For what?" he asks.

"Nothing. Mind your own business, Van Gogh."

He turns back to his drawing. I suddenly feel I will burst if I stay any longer. I hurry to the closet and pull down a jacket.

"I'll be right back. I just have to get the key. I'll be back."

I realize I am apologizing, but I can't stop. I am a traitor. The gifts I give them are filled with lies. When no one remarks on my leaving, I walk out the door. It is a sopping rain. The water covers my face even on the porch. I bend into the wind and jolt down the steps. I am not sure where I am heading. I run to the edge of the lake and feel its pull. I check to see if the manila folder is still there. There is nothing. I tuck into the wind and climb over the rocks. They are thick with congealed life. I balance slowly on each foothold. It is no longer possible to think of dryness. The wind fingers me up and down. I climb the rocks and stand above the lake. I can see for miles into the torrent of rich water and frayed pines. I try to force thoughts of God and nature, but I can remember only not to lose my balance. Suddenly beneath me I see a patch of grass. It is bordered on all sides by the earthy rocks. It is almost a square hole, ten by eight feet. I examine it closely. It is dry and safe. I climb into it, not sure I can get out. The wind is gone. A hollow ringing fills my ears. I look around and see the grass is pressed flat. On the end closest to me there are four or five rubbers. They lie clinging together like the molting of snakes. I bend to the ground and feel its softness. The grass is strangely pure. I cannot think of a finer place for woman and man to join. It is safe and private. The sound of the lake is felt more than heard. Above me, the sky turns in a twist of silk. I can feel the eagerness of loins, the trembling thrust and acceptance. It is a place for a deer to hide.

The wind is waiting when I climb out. I scramble over the rocks and find a path winding up to the woods. Mark's house is a patch of deep brown.

"Hello," I yell, but the word is snatched away. I clatter onto the porch and knock. The door swings open and Roxana takes me in.

"We were going to leave a note. We didn't know if you'd make it over," she says.

"It's not so bad."

"Ha. Look at you. How about some coffee?"

"Thanks."

She is in the kitchen with tremendous speed. I am shivering. A huge fire is flashing in a fieldstone hearth. Its warmth is out of place. The house is furnished too cleanly. There are knickknacks on every flat surface. The chairs sit on four solid legs.

"Mark went into town. He should be right back." She carries coffee.

"You're going to go in this?"

101

"It won't be so bad."

"What's he doing?"

"Oh, he's getting gas and everything. He always likes to be prepared."

"Sounds like a Boy Scout."

She doesn't laugh. She is attractive in the dim light. The gaudiness of the night before is gone. A flannel shirt carries its plaid into her jeans. Her bottom rides high on her hips.

"He left the key. He told me to tell you to leave it under the rock by the canoe."

"Which rock?"

"He said there's one right there. You can't miss it."

"All right. If I have any problem, I'll tell Charlie."

"You won't have any problem."

"You never know."

I cannot relax around her. There is something inside me hoping she will make a play. I do not know what I would do if she did. The coffee is creamy. It needs more sugar, but I can't ask. I am struggling to understand this woman. Mark is too efficient to be gone long.

"Well," I say, "I should let you get ready."

"Oh, I'm all set."

"I guess you're used to this trip by now."

"We come up a lot. It fills the weekend."

"That's something."

We hear Mark's car door slam. He strides in a moment later, bubbling with anticipation. He relishes the two hours behind the wheel.

"Hi, Pete."

"Hi."

"Roxana tell you where to leave the key?"

102

"Yes."

"It's a big old rock. You'll see it."

"I sure appreciate this."

"No problem."

"Well, have a good trip back," I say.

"Good luck fishing. Remember to try those spots I told you about."

"Okay."

I stand and look for a place to set the coffee cup. Roxana takes it and carries it to the kitchen. I hold up the key to Mark and smile.

"Thanks again."

"Don't mention it. So long."

"Bye."

Roxana says something, but I am with the wind. Her voice churns inside. I climb back over the rocks, the key clutched in my palm. I stop to watch a slug climb slowly over a rock, oblivious to the rain. It weaves its antennae at the air, never knowing what it will touch.

11

We have finished *Charlotte's Web, The Wind in the Willows,*
and *Green Eggs and Ham.* We have finished drawing, sewing, and sitting. The fire is turning the metal reddish brown.
Jill is saying something about lunch. It is a day for mugs of
soup and shots of bourbon. We have set out food, trying to
lure the raccoon back. Everything in our small world has
been probed and discarded. We are unable to amuse one
another. Ron says something sharp to Lori and they push at
each other's arms. They do not normally fight, but it at
least passes the time. Jill snaps them to silence. She is the
disciplinarian. She handles all misdemeanors.

"Roooon, stooop it," Lori whines.

"Ron, stop it." It is my turn.

"She started it."

"I did not. You tooook itttt. Stoooop it!"

"Both of you stop it right now. Ron, give her back whatever you took. And, Lori, stop whining."

"I didn't take anything."

"Can't you both just stop it?"

They wiggle in their chairs. The room is a prison. Jill

stands and walks to the kitchen. She is going to cook something to give a structure to our day. It is important to mark time. I want to go back out, but I have no reason to give. It is raining harder. A ground fog cuts off the land at the knees. I stir the fire with a pair of tongs. There is paper work I could be doing for the office.

"Why didn't we bring a TV?" Ron asks.

"Because," I say.

"Why?"

"Because it's a silly thing. It's what people do when they're bored."

"I'm bored."

"You shouldn't be. You have things to do."

"No, I don't."

"Ron, stop testing everyone."

He slips into a small sulk. He whistles softly under his breath. Lori flexes a rabbit nose at him. I try to think of a way to amuse them without involving myself. I will sleep away the afternoon. I will lie with a window open close to my ear and listen to the storm.

"Why don't you both make a camp?" I say.

"A what?" Lori asks.

"Make a camp in the bedroom."

"How?" Ron is becoming interested.

"Easy. You can fix up a rope and hang the bedspreads over it. Then you can put down your sleeping bags and sleep there."

"Do you want to, Ron?" Lori will do whatever he says.

"Maybe in a little while."

"Let's do it now."

"Naw."

"Please?"

"Oh, all right."

They walk off into the bedroom. Ron is hiding his satisfaction. He does not like kids' games. I hear him giving orders to Lori. Bit by bit he is weaving a world around them. He tells her where they are, what they're doing. It is a variation on House. She listens and tries to add more. They are not Indians, but space travelers. They have landed on Mars. Ron is the captain and Lori is a passenger. I do not like their being in space. I want them rooted to the ground, to old myths.

I slip into the kitchen and see Jill setting the table. She is working more slowly than usual. A pot of tomato soup simmers on the stove. She has the skillet warming for grilled cheese. I grab her around the waist and kiss her neck. She endures it for a moment before breaking free to put napkins on the table.

"Why don't we take a nap after lunch?" I ask.

"What about the kids?"

"They'll fall asleep, too."

She comes back to the stove and stirs rapidly. She smears butter on the bread, then wedges hunks of cheese between the slices. The skillet takes the bread and begins to smoke. She turns the flame down to a sliver of blue.

"Well?" I ask.

"I don't know."

"Don't know what?"

"The walls are so thin and there's no lock on the door."

"So?"

"Well, I'd worry about it."

"They know how to knock."

"I couldn't enjoy it if I was worrying."

I wonder how often she does enjoy it. Our sex is a sedative for both of us. We have slept nights together and never touched skin. No excuses are necessary for a good night's sleep; there is always work in the morning. The measure of a man's pleasure is so easily determined. It is hard to know if a woman's shiver is a beginning or end.

"Dad, come look."

Lori leads me off by the hand. Their room is in shambles. A rope stretches from window to bedpost. Two bedspreads tent over top of it. I grumble to my knees and peak inside. It is dark and cool. Ron sits cross-legged, his eyes calm. Lori crawls in beside him and giggles. She knocks the tent a little and it nearly falls. Ron hustles to put it right. They have dragged everything inside. Lori stretches on a pillow to show the comfort.

"This is great," I say.

"It's a space colony," Lori tells me.

"Oh, I thought it was a cowboy's tent."

"No," Ron says sharply.

"Well, since it's not a cowboy's tent, I won't tell you the story I was going to tell you."

"Tell it anyway, Daddy," Lori says.

"Not to space people."

"It doesn't matter," Ron says.

"Well then, do either of you know the story of Paul Bunyan?"

"No."

"No."

"Paul Bunyan was as big as the biggest pine tree around here. Even bigger maybe. He was a lumberjack."

"What's that?" Lori is sitting up.

"It's a guy who cuts trees, stupid," Ron scoffs.

"I'm not stupid."

"No, she's not. It's only stupid not to try to find out things. Anyway, Paul Bunyan had a friend. The friend was an ox. The ox was as big as he was, probably about as big as this house. They were best friends, being big and all. Paul called the ox Babe the Blue Ox. I guess he just called him Babe. They both used to live up here, up in Maine, and they cut down trees all the time. They could cut down more trees in a day than all the lumberjacks in Canada. Paul would cut them and Babe would pull them to the river. Well, one day a big fog came in."

"Like the fog now?" Lori asks.

"No, even bigger. It covered everything. Paul couldn't even see anything, and you know how tall he was. The trouble was, you see, he forgot to close the door to Babe's stall. Now Babe was always hungry and he wandered off to eat. He couldn't find his way back. The fog traveled north, and Babe was locked into it. He couldn't see far enough to get his bearings, so he just kept eating all the way to Canada. He ate almost all the corn and hay in Quebec. The walking he was doing made him even hungrier than usual. Now, Paul Bunyan was heartbroken. He didn't know where Babe had gone. He followed the tracks, but he started late and couldn't catch up. Everywhere Babe stepped is now a lake, so it wasn't hard to follow. That's the reason there are so many lakes and ponds in Maine and Canada. Anyway, Babe kept going until he was in the Arctic. It got colder and colder and he was getting more and more frozen. At long last, he came to the Arctic Ocean. It was bitter cold. He

108

started to cry because he knew at last that he was completely lost. The tears froze right away. But Babe kept crying and the ice started to form all over his muzzle and head. The ice caked on him and wouldn't fall off. He tried to turn around and start back, but the ice was too thick. It covered his legs and he was forced to lie down. The ice and snow covered him so fast you wouldn't believe it. He became just a huge mountain, a mountain just like all the rest.

"Just about then Paul Bunyan came along. He knew Babe was gone. He saw the tracks leading to the Arctic Ocean and he figured Babe had fallen in. He began crying too, but he pulled his hat down over his eyes so it wouldn't turn to ice. He turned back and started roaming the country. When he dragged his ax, he made rivers and canyons. But all the time he was crying and moaning 'Baaaaaaaabbeee. Baaaaaaaabbeee.' Listen, you can hear it now."

The wind is harp-strong, but it sounds nothing like Babe. It is a low moan. I turn and see Jill standing in the doorway. She holds the spoon so it won't drip. I look and see Lori listening. Ron is robbed of his world. I back out of the tent and feel the strange stiffness in my limbs that age has brought.

"Is that real?" Lori asks.

"Sure it is," I say.

"It is not," Ron tells her.

"Come on, you all, lunch is ready."

Jill leads us to the food. Her spoon glistens in the dull light. It wags ahead like a majorette's baton. I feel hungry for the liquid heat of the soup. I sit in a chair and crack the window. The sound of the storm is suddenly real. It seeps inside and rattles the eating silence. Jill tells me with her

109

eyes to close it. I tell her no. Ron crumbles crackers into his soup. It is a fine dust of Ritz.

"Daddy, will you tell us another story?" Lori asks.

"Maybe later," I tell her.

"That's what I mean."

"Sure, at bedtime."

"Okay."

Lori looks to Ron to share her enthusiasm, but he is calmly eating. Jill looks frazzled. She sips a cup of tea and plays nervously with the tablecloth. It occurs to me that she is worried about the storm. I had not given it a thought. My senses are too long dulled by suburbia. I had forgotten the tin gray water outside our door. It is possible we are in danger. The water could be sent higher and higher until it curls on our porch. We could be forced to climb onto the roof and wave bed sheets at passing helicopters. What has been done once on television can be done again. Disaster is but a news program away.

"Can I finish my sandwich in our tent?" Ron asks.

"Sure."

"Me, too?"

"Sure, go ahead."

They carry their food off in squirrellike arms. I can hear Ron already reconstructing the space colony. Lori volunteers to be Babe to his Paul, but he won't listen. Jill gulps her tea too quickly and half coughs, half chokes. She hasn't eaten. I know she will pick when she puts away the plates.

"Are you worried about the storm?" I ask her.

"A little."

"I don't think you need to be."

"It's just the water out there. It makes me nervous."

"Why don't you go lie down? I'll clean up."

"No, I'm all right. I'd rather be doing something."

"It's going to be brutal if it keeps raining."

"Think it would be any better in town? Maybe we could take the kids to a matinee or something."

"I didn't come all the way up here to watch a matinee."

"Don't get angry."

"I'm not. I just don't want to go to town."

A whoosh of wind smacks against the house. It coils back and snaps forward again like a fly rod. A crashing sound digs at my ears. Lori screams. It is a quick, deadly scream. Ron is yelling on top of it all. Jill gets to the bedroom before I do. She is on her knees and hugging Lori. Ron's eyes are fixed on the window. A blackbird is hanging broken in the shards. Its breast is blue black. The blood is too red to be real. I remember my mother screaming when a swift flew down our chimney. The Irish in her told her it meant death. When we finally caught the bird in a blanket and set it free, she slumped into a chair. A bird in the house means death, she told us. She died a half year later in the bed where we were nursed.

"It's a bird," Jill is saying. "The wind blew it into the window. That's all, honey. That's all it is."

The bird is still moving. I cannot tell if it is still alive or if the wind is merely playing with it. A fine mist comes through the hole. Jill takes Lori into the living room and holds her on her lap. I do not know whether it is age or being a woman that makes Lori timid. Ron is shaken, but something forces him to stay. I move to the window and figure how to push the bird away. I do not want to touch it. I lift a sneaker and wedge it under the bird's neck. With a flick, I send it back outside. I do not look to see it hitting the ground.

"That was neat," Ron says.

"It was, huh?"

"Yeah. It was loud. Do you think it flew into the window or was it the wind?"

"I don't know."

"I thought it was a tree falling."

"Go grab a magazine. We can wedge that in here until we can get it fixed."

"Okay."

I stare out the window. I cannot imagine being caught in a flood or large wind. I cannot imagine being forced to react on an instinctive level. Ron hustles back with a magazine. I tuck the edge into the open frame. The cover left outside flaps back and forth. My hands have taken over.

"I think we ought to drive into town." Jill is standing in the doorway.

"Nonsense."

"I'm serious, Peter."

"So am I."

I have not taken my eyes off the window. I will not turn to her. I bend the magazine to wedge it more tightly. If something else happens, I will be ready. It is everything to have something to fight, to prepare for.

"Then I'm going to take the kids," she says.

"No, Ma." Ron is on my side.

"Would you please listen, Jill? Nothing is going to happen. Go take a look at the lake. It hasn't come up the bank an inch. These cabins have been here for ten years, maybe more. Why are you so spooked?"

"I just feel it would be safer."

"Jill . . ."

My mind is clouded. I cannot concentrate on the window. An anger rises in me that has been long coming. For once I let it climb, churning as it goes.

"Jill, I am fucking tired of everything being so goddamned safe! Do you understand? Do you? There's a three-foot wall that separates me from everything. We can't just lock ourselves away forever. It will kill us. You can't have everything safe and orderly and expect to live. There's got to be a little danger. There's got to be something to feel."

I know it is the storm that said it. Jill looks at me queerly. She does not know how to take words when they walk to her naked. I am not sure now if I am right. I don't think the kids are in danger, but I don't know. I have been educated to know, to anticipate. I am a man who knows at breakfast what he will have for dinner. Ron backs away from me. Lori is whimpering by the fire. Jill and I are each a card away from rummy.

"All right, Peter. But I'm going to watch the lake. If it starts to climb, or if anything else happens around here, I'm going to take the kids to town."

"Okay. Okay."

The window is taken care of. I feel foolish in the wake of the anger and hysteria. I would like just once to break something without remorse. I know, too, that it is all a sham. The house is not about to erupt. We are safe, eternally safe. The only threat is from the storm inside us.

12

The wind has died in the night. There is a thickness to the morning air. A thin glint of ice covers everything. It is the first frost, a time of harvest. The lake paws guiltily at the rocks. We have eaten breakfast in a strange silence. Jill has been apologetic as she dodged around the kitchen. Ron has mentioned that the magazine is loose in the windowframe. I cannot take my eyes off the destruction outside. It is as if the land needed the nourishment of fallen branches and the wind provided it. I want to walk across the mist of ice and leave my tracks. I want to pull a pumpkin steaming off a vine.

"Dad, do we have to go?" Ron asks.

We have planned a trip to a country fair. It is essential that the kids see it. It is an American tradition. It has been a pivot of our itinerary since we began thinking of this vacation. We must give our children the smell of manure to carry in their nostrils.

"You'll like it, Ron," I tell him.

"I'd rather go fishing."

"We can get back here this afternoon. It isn't far."

"Can we use the canoe?"

"I want to go in the canoe, too," Lori says.

"We can all go."

"Not me." Jill says it lightly.

"Well, first we have to go to the fair. Don't you want to see the horse pull?" I ask.

"What's that?" Ron is interested.

"They line up the horses and see how much weight they can pull."

"How much can they pull?"

"It depends. It depends on the size of the horse, stuff like that."

"What kind are they using?"

"I don't know. Sometimes they use oxen."

"What else is there?" Lori asks.

"There should be a lot of exhibits. You'll be able to see chickens and cows and pigs. All sorts of farm animals."

Breakfast is being rolled up in cellophane sacks. I push away from the table and walk to the porch. The day could be cut with a knife. I step onto the grass and feel the sogginess. The trees drip and shrug. The light tan of my boots turns a warm brown. Ron clatters down the stairs behind me. Lori follows, a sweater half pulled on over her arms. They run to the lake, anxious to see what has happened. I light a cigarette and suck in the smoke. It is impossible to link myself to the seasons. I cannot remember how many days are left. We are squandering the time we have. Jill pulls the door behind her. I know the dishes are draining near the sink. She refuses to return to a messy house. She cannot go to sleep knowing pans are caked with dinner.

"Oh, it's beautiful." She seems surprised.

"It feels clean, doesn't it?"

"Yes."

"Do you have the directions?"

"Right here."

"You're sure New Hampshire is that close?"

"That's what the directions say."

"Charlie should know, I guess."

"Don't worry. We'll find it."

We both are walking slowly to the lake. There is no memory from the night before to stir us today. Ron is digging at something with his toe. Lori is searching for a discovery of her own. Jill takes my hand and laces her fingers through mine. I can feel her wedding ring rubbing against mine. Two gold bands too hard to cause friction. They slide off each other and grate with the rhythm of our walking.

"You all ready?" Jill asks the kids.

"Yeah."

We turn and head for the car. The lake nods. The sound of the doors slamming is out of place. Ron sighs, trying to annoy us. I back the car slowly onto the dirt road. The tires spread to grip the mud. As soon as we are moving steadily, I light a cigarette. With luck we will hear the Red Sox on the way back.

The Rochester Fair is not a fair at all. It is a carnival stripped from the New Jersey boardwalk and staked out on earth. A roller coaster wheezes through the sunlight. An ancient-looking carny waves us to a parking lot. I know already that I do not have money enough for this place. Lori

116

and Ron are straining in the back seat. Their eyes are filled with rides. I would like to turn around and retreat to the woods.

"Look at that!" Lori is saying.

"We can go on the rides, can't we?" Ron is asking us both.

"We'll see. Maybe a few."

It is close to noon. The fair is just waking. We walk through empty gates and look around. I look back to check the car and see the New Jersey license plates glaring. Papers blow in whirlpools, spinning until they are trapped in corners. I feel taken. It is a tourist trap, an inconvenience. From where we stand we can see the park; it is divided in two. Rides and booths line a large oval track. The dolls given as prizes hold hands in the conspiracy of the con. The hawkers are tattooed. Jill throws a look to me. Ron and Lori are pushing past us. I switch my wallet to my front pocket.

"I think the animal exhibits are over there." Jill points.

"Where?"

"In those sheds."

"Let's go see them," I tell the kids.

They give in reluctantly. The movement of the rides has mesmerized them. A beer-gutted man wearing a change apron tells us to take a chance. We veer to the stables and duck inside. It is dark and fragrant. It is impossible at first to see the animals. Ron runs ahead and scouts the pens. Three large cows are lying on their stomachs. Their teeth work in a sideways chew. I cannot see how enormous they are until Lori stands beside one. Even laying down, they dwarf her. Their heads are larger than her torso.

117

"What kind of cows are they?" Lori asks.

"I don't know," I say.

"They're big."

"They sure are."

"They're incredible," Jill says.

I cannot take my eyes off them. Their hips are huge curves of flesh. The dusky smell flows from them. I want to lay my hand on their skin, to feel it shudder as if from a fly. A young girl rakes hay in front of them. She has a lifetime of experience to block her fear. Her skin is red with acne. There is a 4-H button on the strap of her overalls.

Ron is pushing farther ahead. He darts out of the stable into the sunlight. The stables are connected by open doors spaced a few feet apart. He is already deep into the next one before we have left the cows.

"Let's go, Lori," Jill says.

We follow Ron. The next stable has a different smell. It is lighter and fresher. We find Ron staring at a small group of 4-H members. They are holding lambs in front of them. The lambs heel like dogs. Now and then they pat the lambs' heads higher. A gray-haired judge carries a clipboard among them. As he approaches, each owner puts his animal through a routine. A PA system squawks from outside. The two worlds of the fair are competing for attention. I cannot make out anything about the lambs. They all are thin and sad-eyed. The judge runs his hands over the groin of the third lamb. He kneads the flesh. He places two fingers on the brow and measures the distance between the eyes. He makes a silken gesture, thanks the owner, and moves on to the next. The process is repeated. He takes ten minutes with each animal. He is a retired man manipulating time. When

118

he is finished with them all, he waves them to parade. They circle slowly, allowing the lambs to show their merits. When they are back in line, he goes to the stable wall and takes down three ribbons. He launches a small explanation for his awards. He talks about the purpose of breeding an animal for these specifications. Several groups of parents shift feet. When he has whittled it down to three, he presents the ribbons. They are taken solemnly. A year's work and grooming are not to be glossed over. He pats the winner and smiles. The owner is a young man, perhaps twenty. He is not embarrassed to be winning over younger people. He is a model to them, his lamb a sculpture.

"Can we go now?" Ron is tired.

"Okay."

"I want to go on the rides."

"Let's look at the other stables."

"Do we have to?" Ron says.

"Yes, we have to."

The next stable is clucking. It is yet another smell. The walls are lined with chicken coops. They throw fierce glances at anything that moves. There are a thousand different colors. I have never thought of chickens as birds before. A small label under each cage names the variety. Lori makes up names for them as we go. A few turkeys and wild partridges make rushing sounds in their cages. It is astonishing to see the variation of a single form. I want to know the need for each, the trait that ruled their existence. I wonder if people are not bred like hounds or chickens. There are bantam people and sitting hens.

There are no more stables. We step out into the carnival and hear the exquisite humanness of the place. It is fuller now. Teen-agers dressed in shorts and T-shirts step by in bare feet. A boy lays his hand flat on his girl friend's ass when she bends over a fountain. It is the full license of summer. Another drops a quarter and picks it up with her toes. Her group laughs. A ride slashes by to the roar of rock-and-roll. Ron hums under his breath. He knows the lyrics as well as any of them. Jill smiles as Lori pulls her toward a ride. I have to find out when the horse pull takes place. Ron drifts away from me. He is ashamed to be with his father. He is a ticking bomb of independence.

"Can we go on that one?" Lori asks.

"You sure you want to?" Jill smiles.

"Yessss."

"All right."

I take my wallet out and try to pay the operator. He thumb-points me to a ticket booth. Ron is now back beside me. I hand him the tickets and he runs off. I have bought only three. I will not allow myself to relax. I will not be part of all that I am.

"Aren't you going on it?" Jill asks.

"I don't feel like it."

"Sure? Come on, it'll be fun."

"No, go ahead. I'll go on the next one."

It is the eggbeater. Chairs fly back and forth at one another. Lori's head is pulled back by the velocity. Her face is stretched and grotesque. Jill wraps an arm around her and squeezes. Ron is in a chair by himself. Two boys in the chair closest to him pretend to spit at him. They laugh uproariously when he ducks. The chairs go even faster. My family pours toward me and then is quickly gone. They fade from me as if in a dream. It is too wild a ride for Lori.

Her hair is a straight wedge behind her. The operator flips a lever and it begins to slow. Her features return to normal. The two boys flip a finger to someone in the crowd.

"How did you like it?" I ask them.

"Neat," Ron says.

"Everything's neat with you, isn't it?"

"Aw, Dad."

"They're going to have the horse pull soon."

"Can't we go on some more?"

"Let's go see the horse pull. Then maybe we'll go on some more."

Lori is thankful for the reprieve. Her eyes are still wide. We drift to the tiny ring near the stables. A huge Morgan stands in a mound of muscle. Two men in overalls are busy leading horses onto the scales. They take them away and run them into the ring. We climb into the stands and wait. The sun is directly in our eyes. The competing drivers call to one another and smoke. The horses wag thin tails over circular rumps.

"I don't get it," Jill says.

"You'll see. They hook the horses to that sled. They have to drag it a certain distance," I say.

"Doesn't it hurt them?"

"I don't know. I don't think so. They have to get a quick pull to start it off. Once it's going, it isn't hard."

"This is stupid," Ron says.

"You won't think so when you see it."

"Yes, I will."

They begin the competition without any visible sign. The first team comes forward. Two men carry a large metal harness between them. A third man drives the two horses.

Their weight pulls him forward. He inches the horses around until they can maneuver the harness over a post fixed to the sled. When the men can fit it on, they give a yell that is echoed by the driver. The horses lunge forward, the metal harness snapping tight behind them. The sled twists for a second, then drags heavily across the ground. When it has gone the required distance, the driver reins in the horses. He looks back over his shoulder as the tractor drags the sled back to the starting point. A judge yells that it was a good pull. It is over as quickly as it started. The next team swings into place. The tractor driver jumps out of his seat and rakes the dirt smooth in front of the sled. Again the harness is lowered. The team is different only in color. Someone near me mentions the teams are sometimes used to pull cars from snowbanks. I watch the horses closer this time. They are quivering despite their tremendous size. They have been trained since birth for this. When the men fit the harness over the post, the horses snap forward in unison. The sled does not budge so easily. They seem to lose their balance backward until their strength overcomes the weight. I can feel my testicles tighten. Then they are moving and the sled bobs across the ground. The judge calls it a good pull, but the driver is obviously upset. He knows they will add more weight for the next pull.

"That's it?" Jill asks.

"That's it."

"I don't understand."

"What?"

"How do they know who wins?"

"They keep going until the teams can't pull the weights."

"Doesn't it hurt the horses?"

122

"I don't think so."

"Can't we go on some more rides?" Ron is at it again.

"You don't think this is more interesting?"

"No."

"I guess you'd rather let kids spit at you."

I regret it as soon as it's said. He winces and puts his foot on the bench in front of him. Jill shakes her head. I am powerless to stop the war. I want him to see the drama, the nobility of human struggle. But it is a farce and I know it as soon as I form the thought. The horse pull is dull by his standards; it is dull by mine. It is only the need to find it interesting that keeps me there. We watch another pull. It is the easiest one yet. The horses continue with the sled until it is almost out of the ring. Their hooves cut melon slices out of the dirt.

"All right, let's go," I say.

"Don't you want to see any more?" Jill asks.

"No, it's okay."

"Why don't we stay at least for a while?"

"I'd rather not."

Lori takes the steps of the bleachers like an old woman. Jill is concerned for me. I see a sign telling us the events of the day. There will be a water-witching demonstration at noon. There will be a demonstration with sheepdogs and afterward people can shear a lamb. I pass the sign and forget it. We flow back into the crowd and head for the rides. I know we will stop for groceries on the way back. We will buy apples from a roadside stand. We will take home a pumpkin to be carved into a jack-o'-lantern.

13

The canoe is a silver dart in the water. The chain rattles as we slide it off. The sun is still full in the sky. There are no life jackets. I tell Ron we will have to stay close to shore. He picks up a paddle and goes to the front. I push and lift the canoe into the water. I dig my paddle into the floor of the lake and pole us away. The paddle is too big for Ron. He paddles quickly, the blade taking shallow slices. I move my stroke from side to side, trying to keep us going straight. We head toward the center before veering to our right. I see the rocks that guard our beach. We circle them slowly. The motion of the paddle is settling. I can see fish coming up. Tiny circles spread everywhere. It is the first stillness of evening.

"Let's go around and pick up Lori," I tell him.

He shifts sides and digs in deeply. The paddle turns in his hands. I watch his triceps straining against the weight. We have momentum now. It is as easy or as hard to paddle as we like. I try to see the hollow among the rocks. It is closed from sight even here. Lori is waiting as we round the

bend. She jumps and squeals when she sees us. Jill is on the
bank with her. She waves and puts down a book. We glide
toward them. I want to tell Ron to be careful of the rocks,
but I keep quiet. I have said too much to him already.

"You guys look great," Jill shouts.

"Hurry, Dad!" Lori squeals.

We swing parallel to the beach. Jill holds the side of the
canoe while Lori climbs in. Her legs are bare and raised in
goose flesh. She giggles nervously. Jill steps into the water
long enough to push us off.

"Be careful," she says.

"We will."

"Can I paddle, Dad?" Lori asks.

"Sure. Can you walk back here? Be careful."

She turns slowly and holds out her hand. We are only ten
feet from shore. I lead her to me and feel the sun on her
skin. She snuggles close. I hold her on my lap and give her
the paddle. Ron looks back and bends over his. Lori tries but
can't do it. We move forward by inches. Lori switches sides
whenever Ron does. Little by little we begin to turn. Ron
cannot keep the canoe straight alone. He looks back and
doubles his efforts. I feel a small wave of satisfaction at
Ron's ineffectiveness. I want him to know his limits.

"Dad, would you paddle? She can't do it," Ron says.

"Let her try. She's trying."

"It's ridiculous."

"Let her try."

We continue in a lazy arc. Ron is breathing hard. I look
back and see Jill smirking on the beach. No doubt we are
cute. Lori is slowly giving up. A fish surfaces near us and

125

disappears in a swirl of water. I am beginning to laugh. I want to take Lori and face her away from Ron. I want to sit in the middle and watch them paddle in different directions.

"Dad! She can't do it!"

"Relax, Ron."

"I don't even want to do it! I hate her!"

"You do not. You're just frustrated."

"She's so stupid. Can't she see how to do it?"

"She's getting the hang of it. Aren't you, Lori?"

"Am I?" she asks.

"Sure."

"She is not. We haven't gone anywhere."

"It seems to me like we're going in a nice circle."

"Dad!"

"All right. Can I paddle awhile, Lori?"

"Here."

I turn us toward the center and drive my paddle deep. We hop forward and start to pick up speed. Jill yells that she is going to start the fire. I wave and make a funny face. We glide out of the small bay and follow the shore. The pines are deep and solid. It is miles across the lake. I try to see into the forest, but it is too green. The sun skids sharply on the water. Lori sits closer to me, her body shaking. I wrap my legs around her and stop paddling. She is life before corruption. I wonder if she will want a man's hand on her ass while she bends over a water fountain.

"Let's turn it around, Ron."

He switches sides and thrashes in uneven strokes. I take the same side and lean into the movement. There is a way to turn the canoe faster, but I can't remember it. We move farther out into the lake. There are small waves hitting us

126

broadside. Once or twice the canoe shifts as if to go over. It makes me clutch Lori closer. It is the feeling of taking a last step which isn't there. A minute later we are back in the bay. Jill is bending over a small hole, lighting matches. We drive the canoe up onto the bank and climb out. I pull it all the way up and wedge rocks behind it. Even after such a short while it is good to have land beneath us.

"How are you doing?" I ask.

"Okay. Was it fun?"

"Yes," Lori says.

"You were pretty good," Jill tells Ron.

"No, I wasn't."

"Yes, you were. You did fine."

"I did not!" He nearly screams the last word.

"Ron, you quit being such a baby. I'm tired of it."

Jill has said this. Ron looks at her in disbelief. She ignores him and bends back over the fire. He stamps off and begins skipping rocks on the water. Lori starts after him, then stops. I know she is afraid of him. His anger spreads over the wind. Jill pulls Lori close and tells her to get twigs and dry grass. We are going to have a campfire. We are going to hold hot dogs over yellow flames. It is all an abbreviated clambake. We will wait until Charlie and his family come up to really celebrate. I watch Lori and see the chasm opening between son and daughter. Lori is calm and malleable. She is reasonable because she lives within our reason. Ron is already beyond us. He is impossible to hold. He is waiting for proof that his dreams don't lie. I envy him his anger and turmoil. It is open, clean, and young.

"Do you want to bring over some of the wood?" Jill asks.

"Sure. You want me to make the fire?"

"No, thanks. Actually I'm enjoying it. I feel like a Girl Scout."

"I'll give you a badge."

"I'll just take the wood."

"Hey, Ron," I yell, "how about bringing out some sleeping bags to sit on?"

"All right."

He is glad to be invited back into the circle. He walks moodily to the porch and lets the door slam behind him. Lori carries small fistfuls of twigs to Jill. An old piece of paper is stuck between the branches. Jill doesn't notice it. She feeds it to the fire and the fire doesn't alter. I lift two logs and carry them back. My poems are gone. I can feel the past splintering. It is no longer important to pretend I could have been more. I am an accountant in a firm. I audit the profits of other men's lives.

"How's that?" Jill sits back.

"That's a good fire, Mom," Lori says.

"Oxygen, fuel, and heat: the elements of fire."

"And what are the Greek elements?" I ask.

"What do you mean?"

"The Greeks thought the world consisted of three elements. What were they?"

"Oh, jeez, it's been awhile. Fire, water, and—and I don't know."

"Air," I say, not sure I'm right.

"You're going to quiz me, huh? All right, how about this one. What is the capital of North Dakota?"

"Bismarck."

"Good. Michigan?"

"Lansing. How about Montana?" I ask her.

"Topeka. Now wait, wait. It's not Topeka, It's Helena. Topeka is Kansas."

"I remember the capitals better than anything else. I used to be able to name all fifty," I say.

"Me, too."

"You know, I used to have a wooden map of the United States. I could take it apart and put it back together in about ten minutes. When I got bored with it, I took it apart and pretended the states were cattle. I was a cowboy, of course. I pushed them all over the floor. I'd yell, 'Get back here, Nebraska.' I think it's strange."

"You're strange."

"I know."

"Well, I used to make my dolls tap dance. I really believed I could get their little wooden feet to count out a rhythm. That might be just as strange."

I twirl an index finger around my ear and point to Jill. Lori laughs. It has been too long since I remembered my wife as a girl. I want to ask her more. I can feel us both searching for stories to spin in front of the kids. We want to show off with our memories, to hold out our childhoods to them. Ron snaps through the door, the sleeping bags over his shoulder. He drags them on the grass and flings them on the ground.

"Ron, did you know your mother had dolls that knew how to tap dance?" I ask him.

"No."

"She did. Want to do me a big favor? Would you rush the growler for me?"

"Why do you always say that?" Jill asks.

"What? Rush the growler?"

129

"Yes."

"I don't know. It's what my Uncle Ed always said. It's an old English way to say, 'get me a beer.' "

"I'll get you one," Lori says.

"Think you can?"

"Sure she can. Get me one, too, sweetheart."

It is getting darker. Ron is sitting in the grass. I stand and spread the sleeping bags out. I know we will try to have sing-alongs. We will do everything we are supposed to do around a campfire. Jill runs inside to get the food. I watch her ass. It is softer than it used to be. Her legs have bubbles of cellulite creeping up the thighs. Her breasts have swelled and stretched. She has lost her shape to our children.

"Ron, why were you so angry?" I ask.

"I wasn't."

"Yes, you were. You even said you hated Lori. That isn't very nice."

"So?"

"So? Listen to me. I don't want to yell or anything like that, but you're getting to be pretty smart to all of us. Do you understand? It isn't funny and it isn't cool. We love you, so there's no reason to hurt us. Maybe you don't always see how we love you, but we do. When we get angry, it's because you're hurting us, and you're hurting yourself. You know what I mean?"

"Yes."

"So from now on I want you to try to stop it. I know you get angry easily, but you can control it if you want."

"All right."

"Now why don't you come over and sit on the blanket? You must be getting cold."

130

"I'm okay."

"Come on, Ron."

He moves over to the farthest edge of the sleeping bag. His eyes are locked on the fire. I try to remember how many days we have left. It is not enough time to know my son.

Dinner is over and the kids are in bed. I light a cigarette and throw the match to the fire. I can see the smoke rise above me; then it is gone. A coldness spills in off the lake. I tilt the beer sharply and taste the final sip. The bottom of the bottle slips back into the groove of sand. I feel my bladder swelling. It is a heavy weight in my abdomen. I stand and walk to the pines. I could stumble and fall and sleep face down in the weeds. I would like the feel of something green against my cheek. I open my fly and let a stream of urine run on the bark of a tree. There is something sacred about pissing on the earth. I imagine a shiver of energy running up the column of urine and entering my body. I finish easily and stand for a moment looking up. The sky is a blue distance. The treetops spin, dancing within a gust of wind. I know for an instant that death is a bird flapping through a windless sky.

I cross back to the blankets and lie down. I smoke the cigarette to the filter, then flick it away. My mind roams in acute angles. The faces of the past linger in the present. I can see the translucent skin of my mother's final days. I can hear her rasping breath. I remember the whispered words, the doctor's final authority. "Is she in pain?" we asked. We took his word for knowledge, though he stood breathing and sweating in front of us. He could not know the dying. My father looked on, the question posed and answered. He could not know if her death would be a prison or a liberty. The week after, he spent three days at the race track alone. My sisters mumbled something about respect and time. But I knew he had had a taste of gambling and loved the sweet, sick taste of defeat.

I want another cigarette, but it will cloud my mind. I try to imagine what Ron will remember of me. I wonder how it can be that his memories will differ from mine. I have placed both my children in the suburbs, neither town nor country. They are already growing with torn allegiances. I remember creeping through the backyard of our house in Baltimore. It was long before New Jersey. A rabbit stood in the middle of our stretch of green. I crept closer and closer until I could see every detail of its body. I picked up a stone and raised it. I knew I could hit it, knew I would enjoy the streak of blood on its coal gray fur. Then there was a clap and my grandfather was standing on the porch. The rabbit was gone.

"Peter?"

"Hmmmm?"

"Peter."

A warm hand brushes back my hair. Jill is bending over me. She has a new nightgown that is slit to her waist. Her breasts are held up to me by a palm of bra. She stands away for a moment and loads a log on the fire. She stirs it and brings it to light. She stands so I must look through the flames to see her. I am to be consumed with lust. I must move to her and make love on the sand. I know her body better than my own. There is no new way to present it.

132

"Do you like it?" she asks.

"Yes."

"I bought it for up here. You don't mind, do you?"

"Of course not."

"Were you asleep?"

"No."

"Are you sure? We don't have to do anything."

"Then why did you come out here, dressed like that?"

"I . . . I just thought you'd like to look."

"Jill, come here."

"No, I didn't mean to force you. I don't want to force you to do anything."

"You're not."

"Peter, you don't want to make love, do you?"

"I don't know. I can't tell."

"Do you ever think of me? When I'm not with you, I mean?"

"Sure."

"Do you? I don't mean Jill and the kids. I mean me, Jill."

"Yes."

"Do you?"

"Sometimes."

"You don't, do you?"

"I told you. Sometimes."

"Peter." She squats toward me. "Please, tell me what's wrong."

"What's wrong? Nothing's wrong."

"Peter, I didn't buy this nightgown so you'd make love to me. I don't care about that. I bought it so you'd talk to

133

me. You have to talk about it, Peter. I can see you being torn up inside."

"You must have X-ray vision."

"Go ahead. Make jokes. That's what you always do. I'm trying to hold everything together, but I can't. You're not helping me because you're in pain."

"Jill, stop trying to play psychiatrist."

"I'm not playing. You know that, Peter."

"Then what are you doing? What should I tell you? Yes, I do feel a little alone. Yes, I do feel a little trapped. Yes, I wonder what the hell all this is for. I have a mind, but it's not being used. My thoughts are trapped in my mind, my mind in my body, and my body in a world I don't care for. But what the hell does it matter? How am I going to change it?"

"We can change it."

"How? Are you going to tell the kids we can't afford the dentist this year? Are you going to say, "Sorry, Ron, but you must be an ass to think we're going to buy you that baseball mitt?"

"What are you talking about?"

"I'm talking about money, about responsibility, about jobs that choke you to death. Do you know I used to laugh at men like me?"

"So why can't we change it? What's to stop us?"

"Fear. The current."

"If we got into it, we can get out of it."

"How, though? Let me see the plan. Besides, it's more than the rat race. It's just an ache. It's a hollowness."

"Now come on, Peter. You're a little old for that, aren't you? I don't mean too old for aches, but you should see past that. Life isn't some sacred vessel you carry to God or Art or whatever. It's what you make it. I know that sounds like a cliché."

"It is."

"So? What's wrong with clichés?"

"Jill, there's only one thing that makes a man or woman sane. It's devotion. You can be devoted to anything as long as you can never do it in a lifetime. That's why God is so big. It's a riddle that can't be solved. People find truth, peace, whatever you want to call it, in the search, though. But if you devote your life to anything that doesn't occupy you fully, then you're lost. That's why I am. That's why I can't change it."

"You can still find something."

"I have a little. A lot, I guess. I have you all, the kids and everything, but it isn't enough for me. I'm sorry. That's the way I feel."

She moves close to me. Her gown is wet on the hem. I pull her toward me and feel the press of her body. My brain is numb. I have confessed. She lifts up her gown and takes me inside her. It is a warmth unexpected. I touch her breasts, but she pushes my hands away. She leans on them and presses my fingers into the dirt. I could cry, but it is not the moment. I sink deeper and deeper into her, pushing her thighs apart. She shivers from the cold, from me, from life. I sit up and rock with her, my head locked on her chest.

*

14

Ron is miles from me in the other end of the canoe. I glance
at his bobber and then at mine. Perhaps we should have the
hooks deeper, but I don't know the feeding patterns of
trout. Nothing moves. A suck of smoke strikes an old pain
in my chest. My mouth is black from the taste. I can feel
the smoke caked on my gums. A hawk or falcon circles
restlessly above us. It is different from the sea gulls that
sometimes come inland to feed. Its wings are stronger, more
sharply pointed. It has the look of a fresh killer. I reel in my
line and check the bait. The worm is perfect. The spine of
metal runs stiff through its body. It is a question mark
turned upside down. Ron is hovered over his pole. It is too
cold to be comfortable. The ripples of the waves are beginning to slow. Far along the shore a fly fisherman waves his
filaments. His arm flails back and forth as his line makes
circles of progress. When it is where he wants it, he begins
again. He waits for the tug of a strike. I cast again. Twenty
yards off, there is the answering plunk. I see the bobber
shift under the weight of the leader. It settles into position
and hangs close to the water.

"Should we try somewhere else, Dad?"

"I don't know. Do you want to?"

"I don't care."

"I just like being out here. You're the fisherman."

"Let's stay a little longer, okay?"

"Okay by me."

As soon as he is done talking, his line starts to dance. The lake is cut by the tension of the line. He waits for the fish to swallow deeply, then yanks it hard. The fish flaps its tail into the waking daylight. It lifts its head and shakes it. The click of his reel scratches across the water. The tip of the rod is bending close to the canoe. He leads it quickly, struggling to get it into the boat. It is a memory for him.

"Try to lead him over to me," I tell him.

"Can you see him?"

"No, but he's on it. Bring him over. I'll swing him into the boat."

"It feels like he's under it."

"Sometimes they'll rest. Don't worry, he's on it. Wait for him to come out."

"Here he comes."

"Bring him close, I'll grab him."

The line is within reach. I grab for it once and miss. I grab again and the fish is pulled clear of the water. It thrashes back and forth with incredible speed. It is a mingling of vitality and death fear. I drop it on the floor of the canoe and pin it with my foot.

"Can you grab it?" I ask.

"I think so."

"Be careful now. This is when they get away."

He pulls the fish to him. It is lying on its side, panting.

The gills have nothing to pump. When it feels Ron's hand, it begins again. Its body thumps the tin of the boat. Ron follows the line with his hand and stops. He looks down the fish's mouth and turns to me.

"He swallowed the bait," he says.

"They always do on worms."

"How do you get it out?"

"Just pull it."

He shrugs. He holds the fish in one hand and pulls with the other. It won't budge. He pulls harder and the fish turns inside out. The stomach and intestines soak out of its mouth. The gills turn violet. Finally the hook snaps free. The fish is ruined for him. It is still fine to eat, but he is no longer proud. He throws it on the bottom of the canoe and looks at it. I toss him the chain and it lands next to the fish. He does not move to get it. His hands are thick with slime and blood. He starts to wipe them on his pants, then stops.

"Put it on the chain," I tell him.

"How?"

"Just open the clothespinlike thing and put it through his mouth and gills. Then hook the other end onto the canoe and throw it over."

"I don't understand."

"Try it. It's easy."

"Could you do it?" His eyes are pained.

I thread the thing through the gills and buckle it next to the mouth. I hook the far end onto the boat and toss it over. It is gone and dead. It hangs silver in the water.

"Do they all do that?" he asks.

"No."

"What kind was he?"

"A nice brookie. You can tell a brookie by his brown color and the spots on the sides."

"How big was he?"

"Didn't you see him? I thought we were going to have to get out the gaff."

"Dad, how long was he?"

"About eight or nine inches. Brookies are the best eating."

"Why?"

"I don't know. They just are."

He slowly baits his hook again. I turn and watch my bobber. I have had a few bites, but I've been too slow. I give the fish a chance. I know what it is to have hooks waiting. The morning is still dead calm. A few cabins can be seen around the lake. Mark told me all the cabins must be painted earth colors. They are to blend into the forest. The fly fisherman gives a hoot. He is by himself, but he wants to feel the full thrill. He plays the fish with his free hand. His line weaves back and forth, sewing the shoreline.

"Aren't you going to fish anymore?" I ask.

"Yes. I can't get the bait right."

"You didn't like seeing the fish like that, did you?"

"No."

"That's normal. Don't worry about it."

"I didn't mind hitting that one on the rock, but I don't like pulling out their guts."

"Nobody does. If you did, I'd worry about you."

"Do you remember the first fish you killed?"

"No, not really."

"How about anything else? Have you ever killed anything else?"

"Just a bird once. I didn't like it. Some people like to kill things, but they're the stupid ones. Good hunters and fishermen try to kill cleanly."

"How about in war and stuff?"

"War's different, so they say. You have to understand people can be cruel. You know kids that try to kill birds and things just for the heck of it, don't you?"

"Yep. John Weigman's like that."

"Those kinds of people are angry. They hate something inside themselves. When they kill something, it gives them a good feeling. I guess they can't help it. You shouldn't blame them."

"Our teacher says anything we do to other people will come back to us. If we're mean, then something mean will happen. You think that's true?"

"Could be."

"I'm mean a lot, aren't I?"

"No."

"I think I am. I'm mean to Lori. I'm even mean to you sometimes."

"How?"

"I act like I don't care or that I'm angry. And when you tell me things, sometimes I ignore them even when I know they're right."

"Everyone does that. You always have to push your parents away a little. I'm sure there will be times when you hate me, but that's all right. Everyone goes through it. You're going through part of it right now."

"I am?"

"Sure. You didn't like being with us at the fair yesterday, did you?"

140

"No."

"That's normal, see? You're starting to want to stand on your own. That's the toughest job of a parent. To let you stand on your own."

My line suddenly bobs. I am thankful for it, glad to stop babbling. I cannot tell if I've reached him. I am amazed at my own speech, my simplification. It is not easy, I want to tell him. It is never easy and anyone who pretends to have answers should be avoided. I wonder why I am so concerned with values. I am building a fence around him. I will cut him and prune him until he is a well-shaped bush on a suburban lawn.

The fish is a quiver. I can feel it in my hands, my groin. An ancient rightness takes over. It is a small game played out to tremendous proportions. It is a subtle gamble, chess come alive. Yet the rod is too large, the line too thick. He has the worm in his liver. There is no way for him to shake it, no way for me to lose. I snap him into the boat. It is the same ending; it is already old. I pull the hook out of his mouth and am surprised to see the stomach stay intact. I pull up the chain and it sounds like an anchor. I buckle the fish on it and throw him back into the lake. The silence is everywhere. I watch Ron, hoping he gets another fish. He is one fish away from the automatic killing that must come. I will show him how to clean them when we get to shore. I will let him run his fingernail alone the spine of each, digging away the excrement and tissue.

"I'm hungry," he says.

"Do you want to go in?"

"No, not yet."

"I think they're starting to come up. Let's fish for another half hour or so. Then we'll see how we feel, okay?"

"Okay."

The new sun is just climbing through the branches of the trees. I think ahead, planning the day. I must fill the time that is always waiting. There is a deadline to this vacation creeping toward me. We are already well into the first week. It must be Wednesday or Thursday. I know I could calculate it, but I force it back in my mind. Charlie will be up soon. We will drink beer and laugh and poke fun at our wives. He will fill me in on the work I've missed. We will return in a caravan to fifty weeks of work.

"Want to go in now?" I ask.

"You want to?"

"I think so. Yeah, I do."

"Me, too."

"All right, let's go."

We lay the rods on the floor of the canoe and pick up our paddles. The sun is a track of lights to our bay. We paddle slowly, afraid to disturb the morning. When we reach the bay we see the raccoon in our yard. It is picking up twigs from the fire. We ship our paddles and rock in the troughs. Its fur is the color of dead pine needles. Without noticing us, it carries something to the water. It dips it quickly and brings it to his mouth. It eats it sitting on its haunches, more like a squirrel than a dog. The wind puffs and carries our scent to it. It squares at the water, then shuffles off. Ron watches after it long after it's gone. We beach the canoe and pull it up. I throw the fish on the bank. I want to leave them for the raccoon, but it would be wasteful. I take out my knife and feel the blade.

142

"Let's clean them," I say.

"All right."

We lay them on a large rock. They are still slimy, more of the water than the land. I hand Ron the knife and tell him to slit their stomachs. He takes a deep breath and begins to run the knife down the first one's body. It slips away and slithers to the ground. He picks it up and cuts too deep. The blade grates on the rock beneath it. Finally he gets it right. He pulls the two sides apart like a man separating the pages of a book.

"Now just scoop the gunk out," I say.

"How?"

"With your fingers. Just get everything out."

"Like this?"

He pulls the intestines out. They flop on the ground, pink and moist. He inches his fingers down the spine, driving the excrement toward the head.

"Now cut off the head. We should have done that first."

"Why?"

"Why what?"

"Why cut off the heads?"

"Because we don't eat the heads."

"Okay."

He cuts off the head and holds it in his palm. I intentionally let him hold it longer than necessary. He wants to know what to do with it.

"Just throw it into the lake. Throw it far enough so it won't float back on the beach."

He wheels and throws. He is breathing too deeply. The head causes a small ripple on the edge of our bay. I cannot hear its splash. I imagine it spinning to the bottom, its eyes a cold stare. I want to tell him that's all there is to it. But there is more and he knows it. He picks up the next one and butchers it smoothly. He throws the second head farther than the first.

"Peter, I'm going into town for a while. I'm taking Lori."

She stands in front of me, dressed for shopping. She carries a purse in her left hand. Lori stands beside her, a miniature version. Her shoes have been cleaned with a damp cloth. They both must look new to buy new.

"Do you need any money?" I ask.

"No, I've got plenty."

"Would you pick up some beer? We're almost out."

"Sure. Do you need anything else?"

"No, I can't think of anything."

"Oh"—she reminds herself—"what do you want to do about the lobsters?"

"Do you feel like it tonight?"

"Not really. Of course, I could always eat it."

"Why don't we have it tomorrow then? That way we could kind of plan around it."

"All right."

"Okay. Ron, do you want to go?"

"Nope."

"Then it's just us guys," I smile. "We'll see you later."

"Bye."

They march off. Jill fumbles in her purse for the keys. She jangles them out and unlocks the door. Lori scrambles over the seat and waits for Jill to start the engine.

"What do you want to do, Ron?" I ask.

"Nothing."

"We could fish some more."

"I don't want to right now."

The car moves off easily. I watch them go and see another car push past them. It stops short of the house, almost out of view. A young man with long, straight hair swings out of the car. A bottle of wine dangles from his hand. From the other side a girl comes around and knits her arm around his back. They walk into the woods. I know they are going to the cove. They will lie in the afternoon sun and sleep next to the earth. I look at Ron and see he is oblivious to everything. He is reading a book. I glance at the title but forget it as soon as I see it. I decide to wait. I decide to let them get started.

"Dad, what does *prodigious* mean?"

"Large. Big."

"And how about *explicable?*"

"To explain."

"Thanks."

"Don't mention it."

I am in the sun. I am propped in a lawn chair with my belly flopped over a bathing suit. There is a book close at hand that everyone has read. I can't read it. I want a beer, but it is too early. I light a cigarette for something to do. A beetle drones thickly. It jumps from a blade of grass nearby and glides to a patch of dirt. Its body is color. It is raven black, but a creature of sunlight, not of night. I wonder if there is a bird watching it or if it is at all close to death.

"*Extricate*," Ron asks. His eyes don't leave the book.

"To get out of."

145

"Can it mean anything else?"

"Not that I know of. Use it in a sentence."

"We couldn't extricate him from the quicksand."

"That means to get him out of it."

"That isn't different?" he asks.

"It's a different part of speech. It's used as . . . as something different."

"Okay."

"Any more?"

"No, not right now."

"Well, if you don't mind, I'm going to take a walk."

"See ya."

"I'll be back in a minute."

I stand and feel the sun press on me. I am not sure what I intend to do. I walk to the edge of the water and look out. I throw the cigarette on the beach and kick sand over it. I have no feeling about littering. A cigarette butt can only be thrown away. I step into the water and wade to my knees. It freezes my body and leaves my toes brittle. I slosh toward the rocks. Each step uncovers a different world. I remember Thoreau and his pond. I skirt the shoreline, my eyes locked to the water. The slugs are as thick as oil on the rocks. I see small frogs belly-flop into the lake. I am a sound in a silent world. When I reach the drop-off into deep water, I lean against the rocks. It is repulsive to have my legs so close to the dark, unknown world. I think of eels, of territorial bass. Anything could have me before I could jump to safety.

I look back and see Ron. He is flat on his back, the book held above him like an umbrella. His legs are bent and thrown on my chair. I splash a little water on my hands and neck. I dog-paddle into deep water. My hands grope in front of me, feeling for anything and nothing. I swim straight into the lake, listening for the sounds of the two lovers. They will not expect me. I will come at them like some creature from the sea. I will slither over the rocks and enter their garden. I will drape moss and slugs over my chest and stand above them, Poseidon come to claim the virgin.

Something swirls close to my foot. I cannot feel its body. It is only a motion, a swirling of water. I kick again and realize that one foot has felt the other. I hear a woman's voice saying something to the sun. It is warm and bed-lazy. When I reach the tip of the small jetty, I tread water. I am still not sure what I am doing. I know I want to strip them of their innocence. It seems a mission to teach them wariness.

The rocks are warm on my stomach as I inch onto them. When I am safe, I roll over on my back and stretch to the sun. The voices are more distinct now. He is making grunting sounds, but they are sweet and full. I cannot hear her except in the softness his voice takes on. I think about sliding back into the water, but it is too late. I have to do something. I lean into the wind and try to smell them. There is something there, but it can't be named. I spin onto my stomach and crab-crawl up the rocks. I am silence now. I am the unexpected. The rocks are time under my hands. The sound of their mingling increases. They are reaching something little by little. When I am a few yards away, I lie flat on the rocks. My spine sends rivers of attention to my brain. I know already that I won't spring on them. I ask myself what I am defending and I am without answer.

147

It is not Charlie's land or house or even my children. It is my own life, my own inadequacies.

I see a stick hanging between two large boulders. I scuttle to it and pull it close. It is thick and black. The knob that was in the water is covered with slugs. A plan is suddenly clear to me. I crawl closer. I find a spot where I will be hidden but still within reach. It is a nook in the hard rock. I push the stick toward the hole. I move it just enough to make it seem alive. Its head is a mass of glistening slugs. It crawls across the rocks almost by its own power. When it is at the edge, I roll it under my hand like a baker rolling dough. It arches up as if to see better, then ducks back down. I hear a quieting and want to laugh. I roll it again. It springs to life like a lizard doing push-ups.

"Did you see something?" she asks.

"What?"

"I thought I saw something. It looked like a snake."

"There wouldn't be any snakes this close to the water."

"Why?"

"There just wouldn't be."

"Don't snakes get thirsty?" She giggles.

"Sure, but they don't just hang around."

"Yes, they do. Aren't they supposed to like basking on rocks? I swear I think I saw one. Look, okay? Please look."

"Oh, Jesus."

"It'll only take a second."

I yank the stick back and hide it next to me. I can picture his taking a quick look to satisfy her.

"There isn't anything," he says.

"Are you sure?"

"Positive."

"I saw something. It was there. It had a big black head."

"Maybe it's a sea monster. This is how all the Godzilla movies start."

"Come on, Jimmy, stop it."

I can't stop to listen. I am already circling, skirting around the hole. When I am where I imagine their heads to be, I lead out the snake. I know it should be less obvious. I let it dangle near the lip, making them feel its presence. When I am sure she has felt it, I roll it again. There is a quicker silence. I pull the stick back and scramble to my hiding place. I am close to the water. If they come out of the hole, I can get in without their seeing me.

"What's wrong now?"

"Didn't you see it?"

"No, I'm looking at you."

"It was over here now. There was something."

"Oh, would you quit it."

"Go look."

Her voice is a command. He grumbles something and then it is quiet. I imagine his head sticking out like a soldier from a foxhole. I count ten, then slowly dunk into the water. I take a small pebble from the closest rock and lob it toward them. I want them to know they can't find safe places so easily.

"There is something," the girl says loudly.

"I didn't hear anything."

I hear the rustle of denim. I know she is pulling on her clothes. His sounds are slow and seething. I take a deep gulp and swim underwater. I come up just long enough to catch a breath, then frog-dive again. I open my eyes to see the dull light running ropes to the bottom. When I am in the

149

middle of our bay, I roll to the sun. I look at the shore and see Ron hasn't moved. The book seems to decay in his hands. I know that I am in deep summer, only a strong wind from autumn.

15

It is a gray afternoon; the clouds have been pulled in from the ocean. The water is choppy. It cuts at the shore rather than sweeps it. I take out the rocks from behind the canoe and push it to the edge. A fog hangs fifteen yards beyond the inlet. The moon is already up. It is pale white, a ghost to chase the sun out of the sky. Ron clumps down the stairs. He is dressed in a thin slicker. It is bright yellow and crinkles when he walks. I look past him and see that the door is shut. Jill and Lori are not back.

"Do you have the salmon eggs?" I ask.

"Yep."

"Okay."

"How are we going to fish?"

"We can fish off the bottom. Trout will always take a salmon egg off the bottom in the rain."

"It's not raining."

"It might. Anyhow, it looks like it to them."

We push the boat together, both bored, both brooding. We are getting smoother as a team. Ron's first stroke catches the water and throws it back. He turns to apologize but then forgets it. We paddle straight out, snapping the waves as we go. They are larger than they looked from the shore. They reel at us like ducks in a shooting gallery. We row hard to stay in line. I do not know how we would turn in this lake. I think to tell Ron to turn around, but there is nothing onshore. It will be better to spend the evening on water. A wave chucks us under the front and lifts Ron until his paddle is useless. He waits patiently and sinks it when he can. I am beginning to like the exhilaration, the odd rocking of boat and body.

"Should we fish here?" he asks. He is tired already.

"If you want."

"Maybe a little farther?"

"Okay. Not too far, though."

"All right."

He picks up his paddle and starts again. The light has dimmed. The fog clusters around us. I look back and see the house through a haze. The sounds of our paddles are louder than normal. I lay the paddle across my lap and cup my hands. I blow between the thumbs and make an owl cry. It carries too far on the water. Ron starts, then realizes it's me.

"How about here?" I ask.

"Okay."

We put the paddles in and lift our poles. Ron baits his hook quickly and slips off the bobber. He casts lazily. The answering plunk is incredibly loud. I look around and see nothing. The fog is breathing. The air is surprisingly hot. It clogs in my lungs and refuses to come out.

"Aren't you hot in that jacket?" I ask.

"A little."

"You can't sweat in those things. The inside is probably soaked."

"I'm all right."

"Okay. You just look like a traffic cop."

I cast. The boat shifts from under me while the line is still in the air. We are turning to take the waves from the side. I lift my paddle and see Ron holding both sides of the canoe. I dig deeply and turn us to take the water on our prow. Ron still clings to the sides.

"It's pretty choppy, isn't it?" I ask.

"Yep."

"You afraid?"

"No."

Something tugs at my line but darts away. I reel it in and see a long stream of grass hanging from it. I lift it off and cast again. As I flip the bail, I look at my watch. It is almost seven. I decide to fish another half hour.

"Dad?"

"Hmmmm?"

"Isn't it too rough?"

"I don't know. I don't think so. We'll have good fishing."

"It felt like we almost went over."

"No, we're all right."

"It felt like it."

"Do you want to go in?"

"No, not unless you do."

"I don't think it's so bad."

"It made my stomach feel funny."

"Don't tell me you're getting seasick."

"No."

"Do you feel okay now?"

"Yes. We're starting to turn again."

I jolt us back into place. I do not know why I am forcing us to stay out. The fog is thicker. It is no longer even a little yellow from the sun. I can't keep my mind on the fishing. I am enjoying the feel of the fog. It sits on the back of my neck. It is tropical and diseased. I feel a communion with all the men who ever went to sea. I am sharing a tenth of their fear, their courage. The fog creeps across the canoe, severing us. Ron becomes a voice, a motion in stillness. I think of Conrad's narrator's voice speaking from the glow of his cigar. The huge wicker chairs fanned out behind them. I can't remember his name. It is Martin or Marlow, I can't be sure. It is a great richness to have a danger to claim in the safety of age. Ron gives a shudder. We are hanging on the lip of a wave, tottering. I can feel our weight dance back and forth. Finally we slide down in the trough. I right us quickly. We spear each wave as it comes.

"We'd better go in," I tell him.

"Okay."

"It's not going to be easy to turn. Do you think you can turn in your seat?"

"What do you mean?"

"I mean, I'll be the front of the canoe, and you'll be the back. That way we won't have to turn broadside."

"All right."

"You turn first."

He spins slowly. His fear is palpable across the canoe. When his legs are on one side together, he freezes. The slight shift in weight has scared him. He can feel us riding too far to that side.

"Bring your legs around," I yell.

"We're going to turn over."

"No, we won't. Bring your legs around."

He finally swings them to face me. I am shocked that I can't make out his face. It hangs like a silhouette in the fog.

"Now I'm going to turn. Hang on tight. Try to balance me."

"What do you mean?"

"Shift your weight to counterbalance mine. You understand?"

"I think so."

"Here I go."

I spin quickly. There is a sickening heave of weight and we are almost on our side. He has shifted with me. I throw my weight up the inclined side and feel us feather back. I begin to scold him, but I am stopped by the sight before me. The shore is gone. There is nothing to see, nowhere to go. The fog is a land to itself. It carries no breeze, no direction. I can feel the night laughing.

"I can't see the shore," Ron says.

"We just have to follow the waves."

"Why?"

"Because anything in the middle of a lake will eventually end up onshore."

"But how do you know we won't be going toward the middle?"

"We didn't turn around, did we?"

"I don't think so."

"Let's hope not. Either way, though, we should hit land."

I am confused. I know I should be more commanding, more sure. It will do no good to have Ron more afraid.

But there is nothing sure about this slinking blackness. It is a dream, a mist of colorless night.

"Do you see any lights?" I think to ask him before starting.

"No. I don't see anything."

"It's thick, isn't it?"

"Yes."

I am powerless to explain how this has happened. It is shocking to see the order so easily disrupted. I remind myself that I have courted this outcome. I have tailored this situation to fit me.

We cannot tip over. If we do, we will still be lost, still have no direction to strike for. The prospect feeds me my first spoonful of fear. I take up the paddle and place it tentatively in the water. My senses are alive. I have never felt so sharp before. It is a thin edge that, deep inside me, sheds its rust. We move with the waves. They grow larger with each stroke. It is impossible to tell where we are going. The waves could be swirling or merely luring us to the middle. I strain to hear something. I take deep breaths, half thinking I could smell the land. But the land is everywhere, the water is everywhere, and the fog has married the two.

A wave takes us at an angle and skids us across the surface. Ron's end fishtails for a moment, then stops. We sit rocking, our paddles still. In heartbeat rhythms the night descends. Whatever vision there was is gone. We can only follow the waves. The slight levity of the first acceptance is gone. There is nothing foolish or humorous now. It is life-serious, a time of sure movement.

"Ron, listen to me, okay?"

"Yes?"

"We're lost. Do you understand? We should have reached the land by now. I don't know where we are or what direction to take. We can try to paddle in a straight line, but there's no way to tell if we're going straight. Do you understand all that?"

"Yes."

"As long as we're careful in the boat, we'll be all right. There's nothing to be afraid of. If the boat should tip, or anything like that, stay with it. I think it will float. It will float, I mean. Just stay with it, okay? We'll be all right."

"Okay."

"If we reach land, we'll be able to find our way back. We should come on some soon. The lake isn't that big. If we just keep paddling, we'll find something."

He doesn't answer and I know he's petrified. I have spoken with my back to him, the fog a smothering cape. He is more alone than he has ever been before. Suddenly there is a squeal of metal. The fishing line is paying out into the lake. I reach a hand out and take the pole into my lap. I can't do anything with it. I am afraid to take my eyes off the waves. I slip the pole under a seat and forget it. I hope for a second the fish will run aground and serve as an anchor. I don't know if it's an absurd idea. I don't know anything but the press of moisture around me.

Ron is crying. He chokes everything back, afraid to let his voice escape. I want to turn to him, to tell him something, but there is nothing to say.

"It's okay, Ronny. It'll be okay."

I glance at my watch. It is already close to nine. We have been drifting and searching for an hour and a half. It cannot be happening. At any time there will be the beach before us and dinner waiting. But this time the thought brings no assurance. The world is no longer predictable. There is no one to call, no one to consult. There is no way to retreat from what is already on top of us.

Something flaps close to the water. It could be anything. I hold my hands out. They are becoming cramped and cold. I lay the paddle beside me and stick one hand down my pants. My pubic hair is a greenhouse. I tuck my fingers under my testicles and listen to the pulse.

"How are your hands?" I ask.

"Cold."

"Put one down your pants. Do it one at a time. That way you'll always have one good one."

I do not know if he takes my advice or not. I do not know why he should. I am leading him to darkness. The fish runs for something and bangs the tip of the pole against the side. A wind sucks in its breath and suddenly it's still. The water slows. It is still high, but it is softening. I pull my hand out and stick the other one in. It is pointless to paddle.

"You okay, Ron?"

"Yes."

"Let's just keep the boat straight. It doesn't make any sense to paddle if we don't know where we're going."

"Okay."

"Do you hear or see anything?"

"No."

"Look behind you. Anything there?"

"No."

Suddenly the reel screams. The fish is running from some-

158

thing. I listen to it closely. A wave forms off to our left and rolls toward us. I reach for the paddle, but it is too late. We are inching toward it as it sweeps down. It catches us full broadside and tips the sky. I am on the water for a full second before going in. I feel every particle, every molecule before the wetness. I hear Ron scream. It is a birthing cry. It rings out in the night to be cradled in the fog. I thrash at the water. My boots are two weights. The canoe bobs in front of me.

"Ron! Ron?"

"Daaad!"

"Ron, don't swim away from the boat. Where are you?"

"Daaaad. Daaaaad!"

"Where are you?"

"I can't see it. I can't see the boat!" Ron screams.

"Swim to me. Swim to my voice."

"Daaaaad!"

"Over here. I'll keep talking. Where are you? Ron? Ron?"

I duck past the boat and swim toward his voice. I swim with my head up, my eyes bursting in the dark. I don't know how long he can stay up in the water. His clothes will suck him down. I shout to the quiet, to the water. I stop for a second and listen for his splashing. I can't hear him. He is gone. I don't see the canoe behind me. I listen closer. Again there is nothing. I pull my legs up under me and tear at my shoelaces. I tuck into a fetal position and sink. My foot rams against something. I bend my calf and feel the silken touch of the bottom. It is shallow. We are close to the shore. It is the reason the water stilled.

I listen and hear nothing. There is no sound to pull me in

any direction. A roar begins deep in my mind and starts echoing outward. I force myself to calm and try to move carefully. But the roar is deeper. It tears at my throat, finally breaking it into a moan. To silence it, I dive to the bottom and swim with my hands stretched in front of me. I grab at anything that touches me. I am blind to everything but my fingertips. I touch something that feels like the fishing pole, but it might as easily be a twig. My lungs are inhaling on top of themselves. Suddenly I have his jacket. It slips in my hands and I can feel he is dead. There is no answering quiver, no shiver of life.

I follow the jacket until I have his head. I hold it in the crook of my elbow and push off. I do not want to be so rough with him, but I can't neglect the chance that my breath might catch in his lungs. As soon as we are at the top, I place my mouth on his. My breath eases into his throat, but it sticks there. I reach to clear his throat and feel his tongue rolled back. I press it down, smoothing the roughness with my fingers. I blow again into his lungs. For a moment I believe I hear something. I cock my head and realize it is the lapping water slowly gumming the shore. I push his chin up and try again. His neck is flaccid. His body would sink if I took my hand away.

Seconds later we are on the shore. I find that my mind is trying to judge how much time has elapsed. I feel for his pulse with one hand while I continue to breathe for him. He is dead. His body is flesh without blood. He is no longer my son. I rock back on my heels and curse. I scream until the veins in my eyes run in strings beneath my eyelids. A vast emptiness answers me. There is no longer a chance to rationalize. There is nothing to appeal to, nothing to reverse the outcome. I pick up a stick and jab it into my thigh. I know I must feel within the minute to live. I must do away with a lifetime of numbness. I must mark his passing with pain or it will have happened too easily to be real.

Without thought I lift him into my arms and begin to run. Trees and bushes slap at my face. I trip once and land solidly on top of him. His chest gurgles and a small stream of water flows out of his mouth. For an instant I want to pound his chest to remove every trace of the lake from his body.

Again he fits into my arms like a babe. I back through dense sections to protect his face and hands. He cannot be scratched. I will not let him feel anymore. I will not let him be hurt again. He is my son, my child.

His weight in my arms is no comfort. It jars with each step and stumble. The sickening loll of his head halts me. I cannot move. A pine tree just in front of me points long fingers. It is an accusation, a sentencing. In the ripple of wind across its branches I suddenly know that just as I have called him forth in the flesh of my wife, I have killed him also. It was not entirely random, not completely an accident. I took him too far. I used him to give me this pain, silently knowing it was all that could give me life. I have sacrificed him to my own emptiness, asked him to fill something in death he was unable to fill by living.

I run. I do not know if I am thinking clearly. The noise of my legs crashing through the underbrush is deafening. The fog is still around me. The water is still at my side, laughing in curls upon itself. I cannot stop. To stop I would

161

have to act, to think, and I can no longer do either. I am merely alive. I am an animal breaking cover, wondering when the rifle will crack.

The bay looms in front of me. It was not at all far. I slow at the sight of the crowd formed on the tiny beach. There are men in uniforms and Jill is standing wrapped in a blanket. I am halfway to them before they can see me. Jill is the first one running. Her arms reach out, reclaiming what has passed through her body. I avoid her eyes. I feel her nails rip down my face. She slashes me again before I can move, before I can even think I have the right to move. She has pulled Ron away and sunk with him to her knees. I try to speak, but there are no words.

"You did it, you did it, you did it, you stinking bastard!" she screams. "You killed him! You killed him! Oh, my God, my God, you killed him!"

"No, I . . ."

"You killed him! Get away! Get away!"

"Jill, I didn't kill him."

"Yes, you did! You killed him!"

She is weeping, keening, praying to some ancient expected loss. She buries her face in his small chest. Her sobs find no place in me. I cannot ask for forgiveness from her. I do not want forgiveness. I would prefer she tear at my face again and again. I would relish the pain, the new-found feelings. Then everything is smothered by the rough scratch of official blankets. A tobacco-smelling hand hooks over my shoulders. I am led away slowly, patiently. Jill is left to hold Ron, her body slumped on her knees. I know she is praying. I have difficulty knowing only whether it is to Ron or to her forgotten God.

16

Charlie is silent beside me. The priest has come forward to the coffin in a way that is supposed to comfort us. He says there is a wisdom to God's works that we cannot discern. He says the death of a child is always the most difficult thing to accept. But he assures us the child is safe. He spreads his hands and collects us in prayer. Our words pass up to the high ceiling of the church and hang there, pressed against the saints and angels that stare down from the stained windows. I cannot raise my voice with them. I hear Charlie's voice drone through an "Our Father." He reaches an arm to me and threads it through mine. He lets go only to cross himself.

The pallbearers come forth and carry the coffin down the long aisle. There is no weight to the swinging box. We file after them and see the flowers packed into the hearse absorb the black wood. Charlie leads me to his car and opens the door. I think for a moment that Jill has made some mistake in staying home. She needs to see this. She needs the ritual to diminish her grief.

"You okay?" Charlie asks.

"Yes."

"If you need anything, just tell me."

Charlie is uncomfortable. He is too alive to stand so close to death. He wheels the car after the hearse and flicks on the lights. Our procession will not be interrupted except by the gaping hole that waits. There are not many cars anyway. The boy was too young to have a list of friends to mourn him. He will be merely a name mentioned when school opens in a week or two. Perhaps an unwitting teacher will call his name for roll until someone who knows will tell her to stop.

We begin to circle the cemetery slowly. Weathered names stick out at us from cold stones. They are not dead as Ron is dead. They are bones and hair, not the cool flesh I felt cradled in my arms. The hearse stops near a mound of earth. There is a canopy set up to protect us from rain. There is a cloth stretched over the hole, covering the merge of two worlds.

Leaves crush under my feet as I walk. Charlie is close by me, ready to do, to feel for me if called on. He puts his arm lightly around my waist as the flowers are placed over the coffin. A wind stirs and sends a wisp of dirt spraying through the air. The priests takes us in his hands, alive now that he is in his province. He reads to us from the Scriptures, the words trusted for their simplicity. When it is impossible to delay it any longer, the coffin is lowered. I am told to step forward and throw a handful of dirt. It sounds dull on the wind. "From dust to dust," the priest says.

I am saved from the swell of people by Charlie. He leads me back to the car. The driver of the hearse sits on the fender, smoking. He looks away from me as I look toward

164

him. I am back in the car without knowing it. The wind is shut out. I lean forward and hold my hands against my forehead. I am frightened because the numbness has never returned.

"Why don't you take one of these?" Charlie holds out a pill. "I got these a long time ago. They're just a mild sedative."

"No, thanks."

"Go ahead. You need some sleep."

"No, I really don't want anything."

I can't tell him I have to avoid sleep until I know exactly how I have taken this. I have always judged everything. There are enormous stretches of time in front of me. The future does not balance with the past. I stare straight ahead as he wheels the car through the familiar streets. Autumn is complete. Yards are combed with long-handled rakes, the grass settling against itself for long sleep. Stiff telephone wires seem like branches fashioned by men. It is a time of settling, of reckoning. Ron's death is a stopping place. I know I must decide what my life is to be before I enter my home. My eyes must be sure when they look in Jill's. I cannot observe anymore. I must act, once and finally.

"You know, Helen and I were talking the other day. We were saying we've all got to get away sometime this winter. We thought maybe we could go skiing or something. I don't like holing up when it gets cold. A friend of mine was telling me about Park City, Utah. He said it's the best skiing in the country. I know none of us are good, but it might be fun. What do you think?"

"I'm all right, Charlie."

"I was just . . ."

"I'm okay."

He is trying to carry me into the future, to lessen this day by the computation of time. I love him for it, but it is no use. It is impossible to trade this feeling for another.

The house is too quickly in front of us. I am silently grateful there is no reception for those who attended the services. I could not entertain. I could not check to see that glasses are filled, the meat properly cooked. The sympathy would stain everything. I would rather spend energy than to control it and put a face forward with each condolence.

"Thanks, Charlie. Thanks for everything."

"Would you like me to come in? Why don't we have a drink?"

"No. To tell you the truth, I'd rather be alone."

"Are you sure? It just seems like you should have some company."

"I'm okay. I wanted it this way. Thanks again. I'll see you at work."

"I'll call you later."

"All right. I'll speak to you then."

I close the door and walk to the house. There are bikes and toys sliding out of the garage. Jill's mother has seen me get out. She steps to the porch and quiets me with her eyes. Somehow she looks more like Jill than Jill resembles her.

"How was it? Are you all right?" she asks.

"I'm fine. Is Jill awake?"

"No. I gave her a pill about an hour ago. She was watching the clock. She hasn't eaten anything. Why don't you come in and let me fix you something to eat?"

"I'd like to stay out for a while. Call me if she wakes up."

166

"Are you sure?"

"Positive."

"I'll call you," she says weakly, then steps back inside.

I light a cigarette and sit on the steps. I am procrastinating and know it. The decision can be acted on later, but I must make it now. There can be no more trial and error. It is not fair to Jill or Lori. They need me completely or not at all. I know they will take me back if I ask. Only Jill knows I've been away.

I watch two children burrow under a pile of leaves. I knew their names once. I see one stuff a handful of leaves down the other's shirt. They both squeal. I understand that they are the purpose of life. We live, perhaps, only to procreate. I think of Jill lying in bed, hardened, exhausted, her own life suffering from lack of purpose. There is some balance now between us.

The cigarette burns against my knuckles and I throw it away. I stand and walk to the garage. One by one I gather his toys and stack them in a corner. I do not want Lori to play with them. When they are all collected, I drape a tarp over them. I take down an ax and chop the tiny baseball bats into kindling.

Joseph Monninger's work has appeared in *Redbook*, *Glamour* and *McCall's*. A former Peace Corps Volunteer in Upper Volta, West Africa, he now lives with his wife, Amy Short, also a writer, in Providence, Rhode Island.